*For my best friend Jenna – because life
is so rarely what one expects it to be…
and because, no matter what,
there will always be an Us!*

Come and see what's going on at
carriesutton.net

About the author

Carrie is a professional actress who has worked extensively, having trained at Laine Theatre Arts in Surrey and with the National Youth Theatre of Great Britain. Her West End credits include *Cabaret, Sister Act, The Wizard of Oz, Chitty Chitty Bang Bang, Little Women* and *Imagine This*. She appeared in *Kiss Me Kate* for the BBC proms at the Royal Albert Hall, which was televised, gained an Off West End award nomination for her role in *She Loves Me* and has featured in several short films. She has performed in touring productions such as *CATS*, is a seasoned cabaret performer and has worked with leading Shakespearian company Northern Broadsides.

Carrie's first book, *After the Break-Up: A Girl's Guide,* is available from www.bigfinish.com.

Readers' praise for

After the Break-Up: A Girl's Guide
by Carrie Sutton

I bought this book on a friend's recommendation and I am so glad I did. This was sooooo funny and moving. You know the author is writing from the heart and it shows and it makes you feel that it's not just you! Advice for when you need it and comedy taxi stories for when you just need a hug! Brilliant – and I think I may read it again!
  – Pie

Such a brilliant read from cover to cover – Carrie Sutton is an intelligent and witty writer and I can't wait to see if she has anything else in store! Highly recommended to anyone who has been in this situation...
  – gingernj

I read your book about three months ago and I can honestly say that it has changed my life. As I was turning the pages there were so many similarities. I wasn't even married yet (just engaged) and it got me thinking: 'Am I engaged for the sake of being engaged, because I'm at the age where one should be?' Long story short – within four weeks I had left my job, left my fiancé and moved to a different city and I couldn't be happier! I know I did the right thing!

Thank you so much for putting your lessons down onto paper, they made me realise that I shouldn't have a 'to-do list' based on my age, and that things will happen in their own time. Life is too short and I should enjoy the good times and make the most of them.
  – Tink

This book helped me so much after my big break-up. I was engaged, and even though I was the one that initiated the break-up, I felt broken etc. This book makes you realise that even if you were the dumper, it's still ok to be upset over things. I'm so glad I read this book, it made me refocus on myself and start getting back into the swing of being single. A definite must-read for any newly single woman!

– MissT

Just finished reading Carrie Sutton's book and it's fabulous... even 10 months after my break-up it's helped me. It's funny, spoken from the heart and tells you everything you need to know! It's made me realise just how much I have moved on, I am a stronger and happier person and now I know I am not the only one who felt like I did!

Carrie writes in such a wonderful way, it feels like she is one of the girls, chilling on the sofa with you, telling you her gossip. I just needed a glass of wine next to me to make it a full girls' night in! Whether you're newly single or not, this is a great read for any girl! Enjoy!

– lulu

Available now from
www.bigfinish.com

CONTENTS

Plastering Over the Cracks

PROLOGUE

The Woman With the Black Cat

Sitting across from me is a woman with long black hair. She is hobbit-like, with the beady eye of a magpie or raven, and she exudes an air of sagacious wisdom. The mood is darker than I feel it should be, as I stare at the cards laid out on the table between us. A pretty candle is burning, the smell of antiques hangs fug-like in the air and a black cat paces up and down. The woman examines the cards. She draws an expansive breath, furrows her brow a little and looks me square in the eyes.

'You will get a proposal,' she says. 'In fact, there will be two. Don't say yes to the first one.'

I am a little shocked to say the least, but undeterred. I mentally flick through a list of all the men I know – friends, friends of friends, ex-boyfriends, the non-boyfriend – trying to figure out which one of them might, in some strange set of circumstances, propose to me.

I dismiss them all almost immediately.

I can think of no one.

PART ONE
The Morning After

8th April

It's 5.46 am, the morning after.

Yesterday, my world held two distinct possible futures: the one with children and the one without. In reality, those two possibilities have always been there – they are there for everybody, I suppose; nobody knows if they can or will have babies until they try – but we knew that there was a little life inside me, the man who proposed and I, we *knew*. The doctors put it there. I was told I had a good chance.

Today is Sunday. It is over three years since we met; one year since we started trying; six months since the GP told us the vasectomy reversal had failed; five months since the specialist said we could try intra-cytoplasmic sperm injection and that we had very good odds. At four months I believed him. Three months ago, we started the whole process and now it is all over. And I know the carpenter doesn't want this baby. Or any baby for that matter. He has spent the last year telling me so. But he put me through all this anyway, or rather he *let* me go through it.

I sit on the cold bathroom floor, half-dressed, staring at the digital display. *Not Pregnant*. A big part of me knew already. Technically, it is a day too early to test, but we've been fighting and we're due at his mother's today, Easter Sunday, for lunch. I couldn't stand the stress and the waiting any more so I did the test early, and I know it isn't lying. I'd been having cramps towards the end of the week and started bleeding yesterday – nothing very much at all, but I knew. I think back to the sharp pain I got on Wednesday when I reached for something on the top kitchen shelf. Did I do it? Did I *kill* it? I think I even knew when they gave me the little scan of it in there. I was being given a souvenir of 'my baby', the only souvenir I would ever have. A souvenir of my heart, my time and my £6,000. Because that's what it has been. *My* investment: *my* time, *my* tears, *my* heart, *my* body. Not his. Because it is all for me, I am told. All of it. For me. Not for him. Not for *us*, like he said in the beginning. Just for me. And the pressure has been unbearable.

I go back into the bedroom, my stomach still churning. I lie in bed, composing the text I will send to my friends. The girls from my drama group will be particularly upset for me. They'll all wish they had a magic wand to change things if they could and ask if there is anything they can do. But no. There isn't. I used to think that by growing a baby in a lab, by having someone in a white gown, with a speculum of eye-watering proportions and a degree in fertility science, physically sticking it in, it would all work out. How naïve I was. The other day, my best friend came with me to buy my pregnancy tests. She got her lucky 'pregnant' after a year of trying and, somehow, we both felt the luck would transfer to me if I bought the same ones. I didn't like the look of the brand, the test looked mean in the packet. Perhaps I should've bought the pink one instead? At least it looked pretty and would give me the answer in good old-fashioned lines, rather than spelling it out in words.

I can't get back to sleep. I don't want to visit his mother. Not that we don't get on. We do. Very well. We are all she has, unless you count her other child who lives in northern Scotland and only comes down for Christmas. She was there for me when her son started to 'go off the idea' of having a baby. But I just can't face it; there is no small talk left in me. I'm sinking into the bedding and I just want to drift off into another place, the one I imagine exists under the water where everything is soft and safe and silent. I remember years ago, looking down at the river from Waterloo Bridge and thinking I'd like to just get in and go to sleep. It looked so quiet in there and I thought, somehow, if I could just sink into it and float away, everything would feel better. I never thought I'd find myself back at this place, mentally staring at the water, watching it billow beneath me as I wish for the world to go away.

I go online. I visit all the forums, all the websites, asking if anyone got a negative that transformed into a positive overnight. Of course there are women who have. I pray I am one of those people. But in my heart I know I'm not that lucky. The tears come in great, heaving sobs, that I somehow manage to stifle so as not to wake the carpenter – or his son who is asleep in the next room. But my heart is sore and my mind in pieces and I don't know who I am or what I want any more. The carpenter doesn't wake up. I didn't expect him to. He sees and hears nothing obvious. I used to leave his Christmas presents out in the bags they came in, and he wouldn't even notice or think to look in them, not even questioning what they were. I used to find it endearing. Now I find it strange and annoying. And he sleeps on, oblivious.

I remember back to the first tests I did, long before IVF ICSI became the only option. The 'Let's check you out, babes, before I have my nuts put back together' tests. It had felt very premature at the time, but he is a lot older than me and his 'chop' had been done a while before we met. It was something he had said to me from the very beginning: 'If we get together I will want to have a baby with you and I'll need to have a reversal for that, but you are worth it and I want to do that for you and for us.'

And so I found myself swept up in a tornado and dropped into a seat at the Epsom and St Helier University Hospital.

Then

I am waiting for fertility blood tests. There is no point in the carpenter having his vasectomy reversal if I'm not okay. That's what the doctor said, 'We just need to make sure you're okay.'

Why wouldn't I be okay?!

The carpenter has to go ahead and have this reversal right *now*. It's been several years since his vasectomy was done, so it can't be left any longer. It all seems a bit rushed, we've not been together that long, but if it can't be left then it can't be left. And it's a big show of commitment on his part. It means he *intends* to do this, to try for a baby, at some point in our future. It makes me feel safe, somehow, even though it's all been done and arranged without me. But I suppose they're his balls and not mine!

So here am I, nervously waiting to be poked with pins. I've taken a morning off work to do this. My job as a PA to a major theatrical agent is hectic and demanding – but my boss is understanding, too.

I've always hated needles. I remember being chased around the phlebotomy department at Leeds Royal, aged eight, while having diabetes tests. They had to practically pin me down. I did eventually let them take blood, but it could only be achieved by stabbing me sharply in the thumb. I wish I could say my childhood phobia had left me completely.

It's like being at the deli counter in Asda here. I'm number 63. They're on number 40. I'm going to be here forever. I decide to take my pee sample up to the lab to kill some time.

There is nothing more embarrassing and undignified than

walking around with a pot of pee. It has to be the most socially crippling experience in the entire world. I mean it's just not cool, you can't style it out, it's simply horrendous. I skulk along with it hidden up my sleeve, only to drop it on the staircase and have to chase it down an entire flight as it bounces its jovial way down the steps landing at the feet of a startlingly handsome male nurse. True to form, I turn into a clown, make some highly ridiculous comment and hurriedly retrace my steps.

I get back to the 'queue line'. Seriously, that's what they're calling it. A queue line. It's either a queue or a line, it's never *both*. I'd like to take my cap hat off to the person who thought of that one. Perhaps we can go out for a coffee beverage and chat speak about how dire bad the English language has become.

Anyway, I'm back in the queue. Number 41.

I read my doctor's referral for want of anything else to do. *Check Follicle-Stimulating Hormone FSH. Trying to fall pregnant.* What a weird saying, falling pregnant. It's hardly something you fall into. 'I slipped, ooh, now I'm pregnant!'

I wonder what these test results will mean anyway. We can? We can't? Maybe they won't mean anything. I turn to thinking about which colour carpet I'd like for the spare bedroom instead, mentally searching through the rows at UK Carpets. That's much easier to deal with.

Number 42, 43, 44.

God, I'm hungry.

People are now being wheeled down from the wards, and *they* get to push in. Surely they can be dealt with at their bedside? Surely it's one of the *only* perks of being stuck in here? Bedside service. No?

Number 53...

I look up and realise that I've dozed off and have, in fact, been asleep for the last nine numbers. I'm secretly quite pleased about this, and only hope I haven't embarrassed myself with a nodding head. There is a pregnant woman sitting directly opposite me reading a book about babies. They're all over the department, these pregnant people.

Number 54...

That's the lady with the bump and the baby book. I'm pleased she's gone. She looks far too happy and irritatingly vibrant with her lot.

I'm about ready to steal a ticket from someone further up the queue. I look around wondering if anyone old is dropping off. I don't care at this point whether it's off to sleep or off this mortal coil, I JUST WANT THEIR TICKET!

Number 60. Come on. Number 61. Come ON!

62! COME OOOOOOON...

Number 63.

At last! Thank Christ. It's me. I go through to the room where two nurses are going through more latex gloves than a person could ever wish to wear in a lifetime. They stick me with pins and I cry a little bit at first, because I am always scared and still just a touch traumatised from the Leeds Royal Infirmary incident, then I leave and get on with my day.

And when I get them, after all that, the results are fine: thrillingly, boringly, baby-makingly fine. There is nothing wrong with me, so far as they can tell.

So the carpenter goes ahead with the reversal, setting our future in motion, cementing it...

8th April cont.

He is still asleep. I am still crying, although I eventually stop when I can no longer see or breathe, and my eyes feel so tight inside my head that they ache dully in their sockets.

I stare at the top of the curtains, forcing my eyes to refocus. I love those curtains. Beautiful and billowy and exactly what I wanted. My best friend made them for me. The thought of her, my friend, makes me cry again and I don't know why. I want her with me now. I want someone to tell me that it will all be all right.

I realise I am not only crying for this child, I am crying for my relationship too, because a stupid, silly girl inside me is telling me this baby will save us and I so desperately want that girl to be right. I don't want to fail at this all over again. To have to ring and tell everyone that it's all gone wrong again. That not only am I losing this baby but that I'm losing everything else too.

I want to have been right to say yes, when he got down on one knee in the sand...

Then

'Close your eyes if you see something danger!' says the bus driver, as we bump perilously along. The bus screeches past a number of other vehicles and I clench my teeth. There is a constant loud beeping.

'It's the "beep beep" language, pretty lady!' the driver informs me, clocking my fixed and terrified expression. 'Beep, beep, I'm coming. Beep, beep, move over. Beep, beep, I kill you! All normal here!' He laughs slightly maniacally and swerves, grinning, in front of a large truck. We miss it narrowly. I suddenly understand why every vehicle on the road has great silver gouges on its side.

We career along through the centre of Cairo. The houses on either side of this massive inner-city motorway are unrefined and unfinished. It's as if a bomb has gone off, leaving them with half-missing walls, absent roofs and little piles of rubble here and there. You can actually see inside some of the houses and watch people sitting around on their white patio chair sets. There is something else strange too. Every building in the city – even the ones that don't have whole rooms or a full four walls – has, almost without exception, a satellite dish. When we drive past the great pyramids themselves, which sit oddly and incongruously right by the melee that is downtown Giza, I am rather surprised that they too are not sporting the latest satellite dish technology.

Driving off the death route, we pass what looks like an open sewer. The locals are busy tossing the day's rubbish bags in.

'Are all the sewers open like that?' I ask.

'Lady, it is not *sewer*, it is river... or how you say... canal...

Look see, children are swimming in it.'

And sure enough, fifty yards downstream of the floating poo, the bags of rubbish and the body of a bloated and decaying horse, there they are, the local children swimming in the river. I drag my eyes away. I suddenly think of the time my mother got her knickers in a complete twist when she caught my friends and me swimming in the local pond. How sheltered a life we lead back home!

Trying to distract myself from the canal of horrors, I watch the women with their big baskets, on their way home, crossing the road in front of us. They all have a mixture of laundry, shopping, bottled water and live ducks in these baskets, which they carry effortlessly on their heads.

'Do they keep the ducks as pets?' I ask.

'No, lady.' The driver looks at me as if I am mad. 'They are for dinner. Nice with rice.'

The next morning we meet our driver for the day who, despite being told not to deviate from the plan, still manages to sneak us off to an unscheduled stop at his uncle's silk shop.

Having managed to avoid buying anything, but secretly quite enjoying the visit, we head off to our scheduled stop, the Egyptian Museum, and spend the rest of the morning wandering its cool halls. Outside, it is simply scorching and we are glad for even a sticky half-heat. We walk around, taking it all in, delighting in how different it all is from anything else we've seen before, astonished at just how much *gold* there is in that one building! The artefacts of Tutankhamun, along with all the stories, are spellbinding and we leave wanting more. The carpenter seems to have enjoyed it as much as me, which is a bit of a first. I think we might actually get a decent conversation out of it later.

We are taken to a little café for lunch, which once again I'm pretty sure is owned by some family member or other.

I manage to eat a particularly dirty-looking piece of carrot that I've failed to realise isn't cooked. Suspecting this may prove fatal later on, we pay and are taken to a 'reliable stables' to pick up a couple of camels on the way to see the great pyramids. This is something I've always wanted to do and my guard is completely down. I become 'Stupid Tourist'.

I am totally smitten with Jesus the camel, who is yawning and grinning at me. I am hurled up onto the beast's back by a couple of very helpful stablehands who take pictures of my new friend and me, promising to hold onto my camera for safety. The carpenter gets his camel and we are led around the corner. It is only now that the penny starts to drop.

We are brought to a standstill. The cheery owner becomes a lot less cheery and tells us that the two camels plus a tour guide will be over £200 for two hours, without even going into the pyramids. This is almost our entire spending budget. I demand my camera back from the stablehand and speedily stow it away under a hump while deciding what to do. The carpenter says that there is no way we are paying that, but it is left to me to make the proper threats. I try to talk them down, something I am usually very good at, but I am female and I am ignored – and the carpenter is told in no uncertain terms to control his woman. This doesn't sit well with me. I *hate* being ignored, especially by chauvinistic men, whether their culture is entirely different to my own or not.

So I do the only thing I can. I throw myself off the camel. This has the desired effect! I am caught by a panic-stricken young man who gives in quickly, agrees to *our* price and buys us our proper tickets to enter the grounds of the great pyramids too.

The sun is beating down. The camel driver and guide are

making great efforts to smooth out the shaky start. They even have a certain charisma as they impart the facts and fables with enthused authority as I slowly start to crisp. But I now have another more pressing problem. I have started to chafe, much like a male ballet dancer in too tight a jockstrap. This will undoubtedly be terribly funny later, but it is *definitely* not funny right *now*. I am wearing rough linen shorts and a G-string and I fear I will have open welts by the time I get back.

After a while we get off, the camels lurching forwards then backwards in the awkward way that they do to sit down, allowing me to peel myself off. We take some standard forced perspective pictures that make us look like giants against the toy-sized pyramids in the background. The carpenter seems a bit irritated and distant, and I hope he isn't going to be sullen for the rest of the day as we clamber back on the butt-chafing beasts and make our way out of the complex.

We pause at the Sphinx for a proper look and I see the carpenter getting off his camel again. I watch as he trudges over.

'Yeah, we, er, just need to get you off the camel, babes.'

Wondering what the hell could *possibly* have happened now, I reluctantly clamber off Jesus once more, grimacing as I go, landing on my feet in the burning sand.

He turns me round and pushes me forward towards the Sphinx and suddenly everything is in slow motion. I know *exactly* what is coming. I feel a rush of panic surge through my stomach. No, no, no, too soon, not *now*! Not here in the sand at the start of the holiday when it's either made or ruined. Not after only six months, whether you've had your nuts put back together or not! It's too soon. TOO SOON!

But it is also too late. Any words I might have are stuck in my throat, trapped just like me. I turn around and see his hopeful, terrified face, my mind racing. The sun is flaying me and I am so head-achingly hot and sore, panicking and squirming with no idea what to say or do when suddenly, for a moment, I remember another day under the sun, a few months before. There is always a definitive moment when it strikes you that you love someone. For me it was at the top of a cliff in Llandudno.

There was a breeze with a warm smile in it and a hint of salt. The coastline spanned out before us and I felt the joy of it all permeate my skin, infusing me with contentment I only feel by the ocean. We were walking down towards the beach, him limping a little after his horrid vasectomy reversal. I turned to look at him and somehow I just knew. I realised he'd grown on me. It wasn't that I didn't care for him before, but there is always that moment when something changes, shifting from loving feelings to actual love, something sort of cements. Despite coming from wholly different worlds we wanted the same things in life: a relationship, a family, good friends and retention of our individuality. I saw his show of commitment as he winced and I finally trusted him. I was glad the carpenter had come into my life. It's hard to trust someone when you've been hurt before, and my first marriage had taken a while to move past, but living seemed simple and uncomplicated again for the first time in an age. We stopped and looked out at the sea, sharing the sense of calm it instils and my mind drifted, as if tasting the new sensation. I thought how handsome he looked – not classically good-looking – but there was something about him. Black hair with brown eyes, my favourite. Content in my realisation, I took his arm and slowly helped him the remainder of the way down to the beach to set up camp for the afternoon. We settled ourselves on a couple of deckchairs with the paper and an ice cream, and I thought how far we'd come in such a short space of time. My eyes settled on two children digging holes in the sand and in the heat of the almost afternoon sun, I drifted off to sleep...

I come back to myself, my feet scorching through my flip-flops, staring at him. The sun strikes the ring in his hands, the diamonds glinting and blinding me momentarily. It feels too rushed, I think. Then I remember the commitment he's already made to me and, despite having a strange sinking feeling that I put down to nerves, I know what I will say. I rehearse my answer to the question that he hasn't asked yet.

His hat is askew and far too small for him, pushing his ears down comically either side of his head. He looks as white as the ill-fitting hat.

' . Will you marry me?'

I take a huge breath and give him my answer.

'Yes. I will.'

But my voice doesn't sound as convinced as I'd hoped.

He slides the ring onto my finger and I stare down at it, the *almost* proud owner of a new set of diamonds. I can't look at him. I just stare at the ring. The hands don't look like mine; the fingers are swollen and red from the heat, tensely displaying the sparkling band as the camel driver takes our photo.

I know he wants this more than anything in the world. I see how much I mean to him. He says he will walk to the ends of the earth for me, protect me and keep me safe, and I believe him. I try to relax. I try to feel safe in the knowledge that this one won't hurt me because he wants it too much. It is *his* second marriage too, his second chance.

I remember the woman with the long black hair and think, there was *indeed* a proposal.

In a bewildered daze, we return our camels and say

goodbye to our guides, and for some reason, as I land in the back seat of the car, I cannot feel my discomfort any more. I feel strange and disconnected, as if sleep-inducing drugs are about to take me under. But there *is* something bubbling away underneath all that. A hint of excitement maybe? A sense of possibility?

The sunset that night is even more beautiful than that on the first. I take it in, listening once again to the evening call to prayer. It is calming and mesmeric. The heat is easier now, sleepy and lazy, and I feel happier in my mind. But I still have an unsettled edge in my belly, a little twist that knots itself quietly. I hope I am not getting ill, the dreaded Egyptian belly.

It must have been that piece of raw carrot.

It's 6.32 am, and I am still staring at the curtains. I have written the text to my friends. It's ready to send but it is still early and the rest of the world is sleeping. I can't sleep, so I just stare. What will happen now? I don't wake him because once I tell him then it's real. I can't hide from it. I don't want him to say 'Sorry babes, I guess that's it then.' Because that is what I think he will say. It is what he's said he will say.

I remember all the testing again, the treatment, how long and tedious and trying its all been. It started before I even loved him. How did we get here, to this place, where I don't truly trust him? Egypt, proposals and promises of children feel like a lifetime ago. The carpenter seems like a different person to me now, and our wedding day and honeymoon like very distant memories. How, why, is it so terribly, *terribly* hard?

Our wedding day was lovely. There and then, in that moment I felt like I had my second chance in my hands. It had felt right, everything was real, everything possible, and no one and nothing could destroy it. We promised support, to do our best by each other. I struggle to see where that pledge has gone. The day was blustery and cheery, with the sun shining through and hope in our hearts. I knew I could do this if he was *with* me, along side me for the ride.

But there had been warning signs before the big day. His wobbles, I called them. A bolt out of the blue, huge and shocking. I remember him sitting me down one evening, and well and truly pulling the rug out from under my feet.

Will I 'diversify my career to accommodate him' if we have a child? It doesn't sound like a question so much as a request. I sit stock still, unsure of where this is going. Accommodate him? What does he mean, *accommodate*? Does he mean compromise, share? Of course there would be compromises and I would absolutely stay at home for a time, but surely he understands we must *accommodate* each other? And it's not like he's ever had a problem with how much money I bring in and what it affords us. And what does he mean by *diversify*? Does he really mean give up? Stop working altogether?

'Yes, babes,' he says, looking at the floor, as guilty as sin. I can't quite believe what I'm hearing. He wants me to stay at home for the first five years, and then, once the kid is at school, I can be a standard secretary if I like, nine to five. Oh, and give up the drama group.

I feel numb. It's like he is trying to steal my soul, tie me to the house. My work has been my life. It saved me. It is part of what makes me *me* and I love it. My job is exciting, interesting, challenging. I thrive on it. I don't want to be a secretary or a stay-at-home wife – not that there's anything wrong with either of those things – but that was never part of the plan. I am allowed ambition beyond being a mum. It shouldn't *have* to be one thing or the other. I thought we were on the same page. We're not. He's made rash promises and proposals, not thinking about what doing all this actually *entails*. Now reality is biting him in his new balls.

He doesn't want to be 'too involved' with our child, he says. It's as if I'm ten years old and I've asked for a pet guinea pig. He might as well say, 'Well, only if you clean it out, dear.' But a child is not a pet.

He's done it all before, he says, and who am I to think he'll want to do it all again? The fact that he said he did must have thrown me, I suppose.

His voice starts to fade into the background as I stare past him, a different version of us swimming to the forefront of my mind. It is a beautiful memory, perfectly recorded by my desire. We are sitting exactly as are now, in the not-so-distant past. We are having a wholly different conversation...

'I want to be a dad again, babes. With you.' He whispers it in my ear as our friend's little boy plays trains on the living room floor. 'I want us to be just like this.'

He nuzzles me playfully under the chin, then leaps up like an excited, overgrown puppy and carefully constructs a tunnel out of two abandoned Amazon boxes. The child shrieks with delight and passes his favourite engine through to this new man of mine who takes it on a tour of the table legs before returning it, marking its safe arrival on the other side with an impromptu announcement.

I watch them, smiling. He's trying to impress me and it's definitely working. This is what I want too, a family. I've always wanted one. Someone to love at the end of it all, someone there in my old age calling me 'Mum'. I'm not quite ready for it yet but I am captivated by the moment, and slightly light-headed with the rush of euphoria it has brought to me. Both their faces are alight as they lose themselves in a makeshift world of cardboard tunnels and steam engines...

The two figures playing on the floor start to disappear as my beautiful snapshot melts, leaving me with the now. He is still talking. I am blinking back tears as he tells me how awfully hard it all is, as if I am stupid. He is reading from a piece of paper ripped out from the printer tray, a few lines scrawled on it and rehearsed in my absence.

'Diversify' – a cunning word, one that he does not really mean. He means something else entirely and I feel like I am being tricked. We have gone on in this awful tension for a number of weeks in the lead up to this point. He hasn't wanted to sleep with me, saying he can't get his head around it all. We've only just begun and already it feels like it's over. I feel betrayed and confused. My best friend has said that my desire to have a baby may go away for a while, but not to be fooled. The want will come back. 'Be really sure about marrying him,' she said. 'This is too important.'

I try to grab hold of my sinking heart before it falls clean through the floorboards.

We blundered on some more like this, then I fell ill – and we had lots of time together because I was forced off work for a while. He had me at home, where it seems he prefers me, and everything was suddenly magically better. His wobbles vanished. And I told myself they were merely pre-wedding nerves.

Then

We wander around on the morning of the wedding, enjoying the home-madeness of it all. It is a very different affair from my first wedding and I believe this means the marriage will be too. After all, the two of them couldn't be more different. The first husband was an artist (very talented but very 'up and down', shall we say). This one is a carpenter, a heavy-set, salt-of-the-earth type. He likes the simple things in life and says he likes me just the way I am. He wants a nice, happy, uncomplicated life.

We are having the reception at a stunningly beautiful spot near Old Windsor. It's a tiny little village, completely off the beaten track, and is one of the loveliest places with its crinkled cobbled streets and teahouses. The location alone brings a certain magic with it. The smell of spring is definitely in the air and it fuels me, and my hopeful crossed fingers, as we all pitch in to set things up. There aren't many of us, our families are both small, but everyone has come out for our big day – even the carpenter's sister is down from the Highlands. And we work hard together; we put up a marquee, fill balloons, arrange home-made hand-tied flowers, and butter more bread for sandwiches then I ever want to see again. It's as if we are about to re-enact the barn-raising scene in *Seven Brides for Seven Brothers*. There are mismatching linen tablecloths, iced buns, champagne, Bakewell tarts and bunting. All that is missing is the maypole! It is so pretty and imperfect and we are so proud.

We marry in town, at the Guildhall. I am nervous walking down the aisle but he takes my hand at the end and we grip on to each other for dear life. We are both so scared.

We have so much riding on this, so much blind trust in it, neither of us wanting to get hurt all over again, after what we've each been through.

The service goes smoothly, one screaming baby aside, and the town crier, though drunk as an old turn at Christmas, still manages to get out his 'O yea!' despite clearly having severe vocal nodules. And for that day I *forget*. I forget the carpenter's wobbles... and that little alarm bell.

Now

It is the *actual* morning now. Not the five o'clock on the bathroom floor staring at the mean pregnancy test morning, but the *real* morning when I have to stop pretending that it isn't true and somehow imagine walking through the rest of my life.

He's awake now. We had another fight last night and we are still not talking. Well, *I'm* not. He's trying. And he's sorry. He always is afterwards. He says it was a silly fight, like all the others we've been having recently. I remain silent.

Silly Fights? They are not silly fights. Silly fights do not involve anyone screaming or storming out, or the threat of being left abandoned to a round of IVF! I've had no help with the IVF ICSI. No love, no support, nothing. No husband to come to the embryo transfer with me – I was too embarrassed at the hospital to reveal that I'd come not with my partner but with my neighbour. (Not that I wasn't grateful or didn't want her there, I was glad she came with me; we are great friends. We even go to the same drama group. But I was embarrassed to be there without him, like I wasn't worth anything.) I remember the other couple I saw that day. They stood outside the entrance after their transfer had been done, the sunlight dancing around them. He bent down and kissed her gently, cherishing the moment and all the possibility. Then I went in for mine alone, and had my legs whipped up into stirrups to endure the pain, indignity and the tension of it all by myself.

No one says they don't want a baby in a silly fight. Or

that they think you should, without question, totally give up your career for five years or so because they don't want the 'trauma' of helping you have a balanced life.

I am still silent. I want to throttle him, but the intensity of my hate and pain doesn't even flash across my eyes. He says we should just forget about it and move on. Except I *know* it wasn't a silly fight. I feel like a hopeless, worthless person who no one wants *fully,* and to top it all off I'm still not pregnant with the magical, life-saving baby, even though I had every chance and we were halfway there.

He doesn't know about the baby yet. I stare through him at the plaster on the ceiling that his mate put up there when they both worked for me, the plaster that the carpenter and I fell asleep under several weeks later. Somehow I wish it would transport me back to then and this would all be a dream.

I have been dreaming for days now. Dreams about babies and bumps and bleeding, each time waking up with a racing heart and mind, relieved that it *was* just a dream and that there is still hope.

I tell him. I slip it in alongside something else.

He seems sorry, genuinely upset. It makes me hope and wonder if a part of him wants it really, despite appearances? Of course he maintains it was all for me and not him, but he does seem to feel bad for my loss at least, forgetting that it should be *our* loss.

It is different for me. I can't imagine right now what my future will be like... the one without anyone calling me Mum. My thoughts are whirling. When everyone else is dead and gone, you have your children, right? Is it enough to just have a husband? Perhaps having a husband *would* be enough, perhaps it is just *this* husband? Will it ever feel right again? Will I ever have my baby – the one I thought about constantly before the trying turned to treatment?

Then

Two days after our lovely wedding, we fly out to Lombok via a friend's place in Bangkok. We are jet-lagged upon arrival and, after a quick bite to eat, we hit the hay – the flight and humidity having all but wiped us out.

I wake up during the night and look at the clock in our room. 12.12. I close my eyes but my mind is restless with thoughts of eggs and babies, and I keep jerking awake. I check the clock. 12.13. As I try to get back to sleep, I keep thinking of our journey through the time zones and whether this might have mucked up my ovulation – or if I might already be pregnant.

We haven't had any official results from his vasectomy reversal yet, but I am hopeful that it has worked and we are officially 'trying'. Of course the minute we started trying, *he* started to go off the idea. Although he's attempting to show willing, sex is becoming awkward and functional. There is nothing worse than faked sexual joy, it makes me feel creepy and uneasy. Half the time he can't even manage it, and I feel rejected in terms of feeling attractive *and* in terms of making babies.

We've said we'll give it six months before we check to see if everything is okay, though honestly I can't see how we'll go on pretending to enjoy what should be magical for that long, especially when half the time he's trying to avoid it anyway. I'm not really sure where this leaves us, or what I'm supposed to feel. I certainly don't feel excited about it like I should. Partly this is because he tells me he *isn't* excited, nor will he be. It feels as though he is stealing the joy of it from me, and I'm left having to coax him into the bedroom like a cheap tart.

I don't know why he didn't get his tests done three months after the surgery like he was supposed to, though truthfully, for my part, I didn't push him to. The subject was so uncomfortable to talk about that really the best place for it seemed to be well and truly hidden under the living room carpet, along with conversations that are totally off-limits, like: 'What will we *do* if the reversal hasn't worked?'

Half of me thought he just didn't want to go *through* the tests, that he didn't like the idea of having to do it in a cup. The other half of me secretly didn't want to know the results. The possibility of bad news terrified me, so I left it and now we are 'trying'.

I'm a day late, I think. Or am I? I don't know, with the time difference and the travelling. I cross everything and check the clock again. It now says 12.11. I am confused, and it takes me a little while longer before I realise that, no, we're not going backwards in time. I've been looking at the temperature gauge on the Champagne fridge.

The next morning, we wake up to an empty house. My friend and her husband are at work and her son is out with the nanny. No period yet. I am cheerful. The carpenter is being lovely. It seems that gaining some distance from real life and baby talk is a tonic.

We head out into the sticky air to take in some sights, following the river, drinking water almost continuously as we go. It is roasting and the humidity is crazy. My hair has gained more volume than I thought possible. I've been to humid places before where my hair refused to be straightened, hanging in shaggy curls – or, once, a very frizzy triangle – but this is something else. I look like one of the Shirelles.

We head down to Chinatown for food and enjoy a couple of hours wandering its streets – vivid, bright and teeming with life. There is something interesting on every corner:

a food stall, a shoeshine place or hidden temple. It is such a feast for my tired eyes and I feel a little drunk on it somehow, incurably happy. I buy souvenir chopsticks and a pair of flip-flops that don't really fit, and I can't help but notice the signs, advertising all manner of massage, hanging above almost every doorway. I realise that, in complete contrast to similar doorways on the streets of London, these places are offering *actual* massages rather than veiling themselves with the misleading title of 'Stress Relief.' I nip inside one such place, leaving the carpenter perusing fisherman's pants – he doesn't want to indulge – and I come out an hour later looking exquisitely doped up. I am a walking high, no drugs needed.

At the end of the day, we regroup with my friend, who treats us to drinks at the top of the Banyan Tree hotel, in the Vertigo and Moon Bar, boasting the best views in all of Bangkok. The sunset is wearing its most glorious coat of orange, pink and gold and we watch the horizon, all of us hushed, as the sun drops out of sight. For the briefest of moments the world hangs suspended in time. The carpenter looks at me, eyes smiling, as we share the perfect stillness. Perhaps we *are* on the same page? I almost daren't breathe. He seems happy. Content. Calm. Mine...

And then the moment is broken as we are pulled away to go and eat.

The next morning I play with my friend's son. He is a sweet little thing and I wonder what my son might look like. Will he be dark and brooding like the carpenter or stubbornly red-headed like me? The boy serves some 'air' tea and offers me some hot yogurt, which I pretend to eat and discard quickly, before we head off for brunch and a quick whizz round the botanical gardens before catching our flight out. The gardens are, in feel, somewhere between those at Kew and the jungle. I see chipmunks darting about the place and I am instantly quite giddy. The carpenter hates animals, but I've always been an idiot for them.

We walk slowly. The heat is worse today but we don't let it spoil things. We take in the waterfall, the gardens of ginger, a pretty lake and then, as we round a corner, a veritable fairy dell filled to brimming with orchids of every kind and colour imaginable. It is sheer enchantment. I just want to fill it with butterflies, fairies and a few flying My Little Ponies. The two hours we spend here are lazy and delicious; we feel in love. And somewhere in the heat and dizzying scent of the place he takes my hand, kisses it gently and leads me on...

When we travel on to Lombok and the blood comes, I know, again, that I am not pregnant. I gingerly tell him what has happened, trying to keep it light so as to not let it spoil things, making a mental note of the rough dates then putting it out of reach again in the back of my mind. We are getting on so much better and I don't want the talk of babies to upset things again.

We have organised a private excursion with a local guide who, it turns out, is into amateur dramatics and performs every other night in the kecak play. I tell him that I perform with a drama group back at home and we chat about our shared interest for a while as the carpenter looks out of the window. He has started to resent my hobby of late, getting less and less accepting of the Tuesday and Thursday evenings I spend away from the house. I've suggested he might use the opportunity to take his son out on one of these nights. *Do* something with the time for himself. But it seems he'd rather sit in missing me than get off his backside and *live*. It is a subject that we've left alone for the time being. I won't back down and give it up and he refuses to accept it, so we're at a stalemate of sorts.

As we drive through the countryside, our guide giving us his interesting running commentary, I am quite shocked to see some old ladies wearing open-fronted dresses. Their sagging breasts are swinging around for all to see, but the guide tells me that this is their way and that many of the villagers still wear traditional attire. Some of them still believe that they are invisible when bathing nude in rivers. I decide this is a splendid form of denial and wonder if it'd pass as a reasonable excuse if I ever fancied skinny-dipping in the Hyde Park lido. You can get away with all sorts in the name of culture or religion these days. It might be an interesting experiment.

We arrive at a Tirta water temple. It is a restful sort of place, ancient, with waters that filter through quicksand and come out as pure as pure can be, through a row of spouts set into a walled pool at the other side of the compound. I have a strong urge to join the locals as they make their offerings and bathe in this sacred water, washing their heads, eyes and mouth as they pray. Our guide picks up on this and asks if we would like to have a go at the ritual. I do. The carpenter does not.

I am dressed in a delicate purple sarong and taken to the altar stone to make my offering along with the locals. There are flowers and burning incense sticks everywhere and I am strangely pulled into their world, a feeling of spirituality taking over me as I close my eyes and pray for fate to bring me my baby. *Our* baby. I don't believe in the Christian God who lives in the sky, but perhaps if I pray to *their* gods, believe in this ritual, I will get my wish. So I follow the others as they clean away their demons, pray for forgiveness, pray for their families, friends, babies, loved ones.

The water is welcomingly cool and fresh and I feel safe, clean and peaceful. Protected. The guide tells me to drink some and I do. I am not thinking, I am just doing, following. The water is pure on my tongue. Refreshing. As clear as crystal. It's as if it is cleansing me of my troubles, inside and out, and I let the feeling wash over me as the water rains down my throat and cascades over my head. I complete the ritual slowly, not wanting it to ever be over, and emerge from the flower-laden pool with a grace I haven't felt in a while.

The man, our guide, looks at me, and smiles. 'You two are newlyweds?'

I nod.

'Maybe you make baby in Lombok?'

I tip him.

Now

The carpenter sits up beside me in the bed as the reality of the loss hits me and the tears come again. He says he is sorry. He rubs my arm and puts his head on my shoulder. He says we will try again, but the magic words are lost on me somehow. If only he could have said them months ago, to take away the pressure, give us a real stress-free fighting chance. The pain of now is too great for me to really think beyond this moment and, besides, what if we *do* try again and it still doesn't work? Can I even go through all of this again?

He tries to be sweet. He says some people are on their seventh go, that it can take ages. I want to believe that he is that person who will keep going along this road with me – *with* me, beside me, not following a few feet behind, but fighting for it, fighting for us, trying as many times as it takes, wanting it. But we both know we won't go that far. He says so many things he doesn't mean. There isn't enough money for one thing. We both thought, or hoped, that one round would do it. I'd been ignoring my inner voice that knew better. I'd mentally turned the volume down.

I feel lonely and isolated in my grief. I feel cross with him about the argument the night before. I tell him I'm not going to his mother's. She rings me to get me to go, but I just can't. He thinks I blame him and don't want him near me. It's not *entirely* true. I *want* to be held by him and feel I can trust him with my heart and sorrow, but I'm so angry with him at the same time. I don't blame him for it not working but I *do* blame him for his behaviour. I need to let myself grieve. He has no right to butt in on my grief, after abandoning me to the hardness of the treatment. He doesn't get to play the white knight in shining armour now. He hasn't earned the right.

There are times when I feel trapped in this house. It was meant to be *my* house, *my* happy place, my sanctuary after my first marriage blew up in my face. But I never had any time with it just being mine before the new era of *him* came in. I can't escape here. I can't hide how I feel. It has all been too much; I am inconsolable. I look at my picture, my little scan. And the tears simply won't stop. He goes out, comes home, and goes out again. I get up and watch TV. I have nothing to do but wait until tomorrow. He returns with a bag from the corner shop. I know what's inside.

I go into the bedroom and lie down for a while. When I come out, the carpenter is sitting in his usual position with stained lips and an empty glass. I get angry with him. He's drunk. Any sign of hardship, and he drinks. He fills the blanks in his mind with glasses of red, his crutch firmly in place. I want to shout, 'Don't do this to me today! Don't make this about *you*. I need you here for me, *with* me, and this is what you choose to do?' After everything, he can't even just be here for me without getting pissed. I am furious.

Eventually he tries to hug me and I push him away. I go to the bathroom and sit on the loo, lid down, with my knees pulled into my chest, holding my scan. He finds me, holds me tight and I cry and cry. My hair is soaked through at the front and I feel like my life is over. He gets me up and we go through and cuddle on the sofa. It is not a cuddle I want somehow, but I calm down a little nonetheless. It is better than no cuddles at all.

We watch TV and the magic box pacifies me for a time. I drift off to sleep realising how long I have felt like this for, or at least different shades of *this*. It has eaten away at me, at us: the trying, the attempts and the talking about it.

Then

Three months after our wedding and I am sitting in the shopping centre just down the road from us. I'm watching all the mums and kids go by. It's impossible to escape them at the moment, it's the school holidays and they're out in force. It's safe to say I've felt sick for the last two weeks, and I don't mean in the 'maybe I'm pregnant' way.

We've been 'trying' since before the wedding, in vain it would seem. I'm sick from nerves and the horrid possibility that this might never happen for me. It's not even like I need it to happen right now, I think, I just want to know it *could* happen, or maybe just that he *wants* it to happen. But, for his sake, it needs to be now or it's going to be never. I have no choice but to do it now and it all feels so very, very wrong. We are working to his time frame not mine, and it is a compromise I feel I have to make. His strange, unreasonable deadline is fast approaching, the window of opportunity has all but closed, and it's not even *my* window.

When I got the news, the dreaded news, that the highly expensive reversal had failed, I just sat there. I didn't make a single sound, not one. I don't know that I've ever been truly silent, but in that moment there was nothing. My eyes poured and my throat was tight and I felt utterly empty. I'd just finished my morning's work and was sitting in the main lobby when he called me. I answered the phone with a stone in my stomach and he just blurted it out.

'There's nothing to work with. Sorry babes. I guess that's it.'

That's it? Just like that? What does he mean?

It feels as though someone is squeezing my heart, with

white knuckles and a nasty smile as the pain spreads across my chest. My body feels limp. Everything spins as if I've had a hundred vodkas. My eyes won't focus, my face feels numb and I'm convinced that at any moment I'm going to throw up on my shoes.

People are staring even though I try to hide my face behind sunglasses. My make-up is streaking down my cheeks. Then my favourite work friend comes down the stairs towards me. She doesn't need to say a thing, her being there is enough. She takes me for lunch, holding my hand as she leads me through the crowds to our favourite restaurant. We hide in there until I am calm and no longer blotchy. I tell her what has happened with a strange coolness in my voice. I manage to eat. We talk and even joke a little. It helps. I want so much to be wrong in feeling that things are hopeless. But my gut is nagging away at me.

I ring the doctor for the reversal test results because I don't quite believe the carpenter's version of things. I'm not entirely convinced he wouldn't lie to get me to give up everything, or at least pretend we have no other options. It is worrying that I don't quite *trust* him, and I wonder how long it's been since I did. When I speak to the doctor's receptionist she can make neither head nor tale of the results and is rude and vague – I've always wondered what qualifies a receptionist to give you your results – so I make an appointment to go in that evening.

The carpenter reluctantly agrees to come too – after much convincing, a little crying on my part and a certain amount of shouting at each other. At least I still have a little fight in me. It is complicated, we're told. It is *not* good. They found nothing to work with at all on his side of things. Nada. Not a one. The reversal didn't work, full stop. We can't have a baby naturally. But we do still have some options.

I glare sideways at the carpenter, his dark curls falling

over his face as he stares into his lap. I knew he wasn't giving me the full story. The doctor goes on: we could try a couple of versions of IVF. Both ways would involve retrieving sperm directly from the source, a bit like having a blood test. From there, depending on the numbers they find, we could attempt traditional IVF – where they place each egg in with, say, 100 sperm and see what they get up to – or we could have IVF ICSI, where a single sperm is injected into each viable egg to fertilize it. But we are told we must prepare for the eventuality that they may find nothing. It is possible that it can't be his baby. It is possible that we might need a donor.

The carpenter doesn't seem terribly put out by the failed reversal. He's had a child already, after all, so he knows he 'works', or rather, that he did. He is very open about the reversal with everyone, doesn't seem to care who knows. But I can see his hackles are up at the mention of an even dirtier word than baby: *Donor*.

We are referred to a specialist. He agrees to that at least, with a certain amount of belligerence, but I don't trust him. I am quite sure that at any minute he will adopt some sort of argument to try and rob me of ever being a mummy; I can feel him formulating a plan. The little wobble he had just before the wedding was clearly no wobble at all, and he cannot explain it away this time with a bit of scrawl on a page of paper about 'diversifying' that he pulled from the printer.

So we're at another stalemate. And do you know what? If we can't then we can't. I could live with *can't*, if the love were enough. But this is *doesn't want*. Doesn't want? After what he said in the beginning?

'I want a chance to get to right, babes. I was never the best dad.' It was a summer evening, a few days before his reversal, and we were both a bit drunk, sitting out on the new patio that we'd spent two days painstakingly laying at my place. 'I didn't think about the boy at all most of the time.' He is talking about his son – my stepson – who he has constant guilt about. 'I did what *I* wanted and what was right for me. I never did what was right for him. Or for her.' He means his first wife. 'I just left her at home with the kid all the time. I worked six days a week and when I was at home I just didn't want to know. So I'd go straight upstairs after work, have a bath and then go out again. Or sit and watch telly with a beer. But I was young then... And we never worked like me and you do. I want to make it right and be the best dad I can be. I want a second chance.'

I sat and listened. I tasted the elderflowers coming through in the wine. I closed my eyes.

8th April cont.

The TV is flashing away to itself. The carpenter has nothing to say to me. He just stares at me with blank, watery eyes. There is nothing in them. It's like looking in to the eyes of a dead fish. He gets up and goes out for more alcohol and returns to his position, letting the drink rinse him of sense. His drinking grates on me. It controls him much more than he realises.

He starts to grab at me, not aggressively, but he is fumbling and clutching at me and the smell of the booze, hot and strong on his breath as he drunkenly puts his huge arms around me, makes me feel nauseous. He hugs me again but I feel trapped in his arms now. Not safe, not better, not comforted: trapped. The smell of the sticky, sickly red wine is making me heady and woolly-minded and I can't relax my rigid body. I was calming down, letting him in through a tiny chink in my defences and he ruined it with his clumsy foolishness. I can't forgive him. Not yet. Not now.

I sit, statue-like and stony for the remaining hours until the day finally ends and sleep comes to assuage my tired heart for a time.

9th April

I wake at 5.00am, bursting for the loo, and remember that scrap of hope. I can re-test. I force my bladder to hold it till 8.00am. Waiting, praying, as I cross my legs, I think back to the pool in Lombok, with the flowers floating on the water. The place where I prayed for the baby that would save us.

I take the test. Will I be one of the rare few?

It takes two minutes for the test to work, every second worse than the one before, then there they are again. Those words.

Not Pregnant.

I walk back to bed feeling a bit numb but I am not crying this time. I knew, after all, didn't I? This was just confirmation. I ring the hospital but it is too early. It's bank holiday Monday. No one will be in the assisted conception unit until 9.00am, they tell me. I sit in bed. He sits with me. We wait.

I call back at 9.06am and get Dr Flint. I give her my result. The ever-hopeful part of me says, 'I'm sure you'll want to do a blood test to confirm? Maybe I am one of those rare cases?'

'No,' she says a little too quickly and far too bluntly. 'The tests are so accurate these days, it's pretty conclusive.' She says someone will ring tomorrow with a follow-up appointment. It isn't a long conversation. There is nothing to be done about how horrendous I feel, it's just another day in the office for them. I'm another number, another statistic.

I hang up the phone and the crying comes again. I cannot stop it.

My heart hurts in a thousand places as I put away all my IVF medication. The vitamins. The drugs. The needles. The aspirin. My little scan.

I ask to go swimming. I want to get into the cool water, where it is silent and safe. He says he will take me. In my mind I see the river, but he is unlikely to take me *there*, even if I asked him to, especially if I show signs of actually wanting to get in. And at least I'm unlikely to drown myself in the pool at the Ashley Centre. I need to go now, right away; I want to move. Swimming is one of my favourite things and the IVF had stolen it from me. I want to snatch it back.

He isn't finished doing his jobs yet, so I go and sit in the car, waiting as the persistent rain becomes torrential and beats against the metal. I'm still crying. Ordinarily I hate rain but today is one of the few rare occasions I'm grateful for it. The sound of it drumming down drowns me out, and the sheets in which it is coming mask my face from the passers-by. I am hidden.

We drive in silence and my face is red and puffy when we arrive. The people at the baths will think someone's died. I suppose they have, in a way. It certainly feels like that. My poor little life. Soon nature will kick in and wash him away.

I change in a hurry. The carpenter is not actually getting in with me, he says he'll wait in the café. I don't know whether I really wanted him to swim or not, but it is one more thing he has chosen not to do, something else of himself he hasn't given.

I get into the water... push off... and glide. The water rushes by my face, caressing my hot skin, cooling it, soothing me. I feel weightless, flying through the pool. It is what I need, a few moments of peace.

I stop to rest for a while, and a man talks to me. He's trying to see if he can ask me out. I am polite, but quickly leave. I can't explain myself today. Wishing I could have stayed in the water for longer, I get under the sharp, hot shower, scrubbing my hair until it is far too clean. It's as if I'm trying to scour the truth of it all away. There are two women standing by the mirrors as I try to make myself presentable. They are tapping their feet impatiently as I take my time with the coin-operated hairdryer. They keep rolling their eyes and raising their brows, I'm evidently not going quickly enough for their busy schedules.

I look towards them and think, 'You have a bump, *you* have a baby... I'm getting the hairdryer!'

We go into town and I do feel a bit better. I hope that that was it for the crying and I can now miraculously move on.

We go to Boots and I buy tampons. I also buy folic acid, saying that since we're going to be trying again I'll keep taking it to build up a reserve. I am testing him to see if he meant it when he said we'd have another go. He okays the folic acid. This is good. It feels better to be looking ahead.

We go and have some lunch. The service is awful, so awful that they voluntarily only charge us for one meal. We leave and go to the cinema. I could use an hour or two's distraction but there is nothing terribly good showing, so we don't bother in the end and go home and watch a film there instead.

I make a very average dinner. We watch more telly.

I go to bed alone; he follows some hours later.

10th April

I wake up at 7.00am, grateful at least that it's not 5.00am like it has been. I do not know what I am going to do with myself. I have no job to go to at the moment.

That's another pressure I've had to cope with. He convinced me to take an unpaid sabbatical from work, to focus on the IVF, saying that he'd support me. Then, somewhere mid-cycle, he started hinting that I needed to *get* work as we were struggling for cash. I called the office to see if I could un-arrange things, but they already had another intern in to cover me and it wasn't possible.

It is all so confusing for me. I don't know what is expected of me because it keeps changing. I registered with a marketing company who give out one-off jobs here and there and I'm praying I get something soon, otherwise, how will I occupy myself until we start all this again? I don't know if I will feel better for the wait or just be more stressed that it's taking so long to get to the end of the rainbow. Maybe the carpenter will go off the idea again if we leave it too long? This is a constant worry for me.

It is Tuesday. My parents are on their way down from Leeds to see me. I don't know what time they will arrive, so I'm plodding aimlessly through the day, waiting. The man from John Lewis has been to pick up the third broken kettle we've had to send back in as many months. Why is nothing as reliable as it's meant to be? Expensive treatments? Kettles? Husbands?

The blood still hasn't come properly, so I'm just *waiting*. A small part of my mind still thinks that it won't come at all and I'll be that *mega* miracle girl who was really pregnant all along. Maybe I'll go out and buy a cat? Maybe not. Images of me as a sad old cat lady flash through my mind and I dismiss the idea. Besides, the carpenter's very clear about cats. He hates them, pets in general really. He doesn't like the ties or the responsibility. I don't know *what* I want any more. I can't even choose a new kettle, let alone decide on a pet. Cats will have to wait.

I stare out of the window. Bertie the Bruiser, next door's cat, takes a swipe at a passing squirrel. He misses and I'm pleased. His doesn't *always* miss. I remember him once, trotting up the garden path like a mini panther, with a particularly fat one dangling by its throat. I couldn't believe that he'd even managed to catch the bloody thing, let alone that it was still alive! I ran outside, clapping and screeching to make the cat jump. Bertie dropped the squirrel, which legged it up the nearest tree, leaving the cat eyeballing me. Some time later that day, he left a squirrel's head on my doormat, like some Cat Mafia calling card, as if to teach me a lesson.

I am busy reliving this when my parents' faces pop up at the window. My mum has brought me a gift, a new perfume. A consolation prize. They come in, trying to be cheery, and hug me. There is nothing much to say.

Later...

I think this whole process may actually send me round the twist. Tonight, I finally lost it. I actually went nuts. Completely and utterly nuts. It hadn't been a good day, in fairness. The rain had been throwing itself down on us for hours, mum and dad and me. We'd driven over to Old Windsor and squelched around all afternoon. I retraced the steps I took to the Guildhall the day I married the carpenter. I remembered how I'd gathered quite a parade by the time I got to the beautiful old building itself. There's nothing like a blushing bride to attract a crowd.

We pass a big church, and Mum and I go in. Despite being an atheist, something about the smell and age of places like this, the number of people who have prayed on their knees over the years who are still there in spirit somehow, makes them feel safe and welcoming to me. I've always felt at home in them, perhaps because ultimately churches represent what we should all try to be: good. Today I go in because I don't feel safe any more. I have no control over where my future will take me. I had thought it was all mapped out and that, in a strange hotchpotch sort of way, it was coming together. But not any more. I was prepared for it to be *hard*, but I wasn't prepared for this.

I light candles at the church, one for each of my little lives: the one we put back and the one we didn't. Then I light one for me. I wait for the flames to take hold, watching them flicker in the dim light of the place. I try to take in the ambience but my mood is dark again and I can't shift it. There is little comfort in it today.

The rain that stopped while we were inside starts to fall again as we leave, as if on cue. We wander in and out of the little shops, essentially killing time, but by the time we get down to the bottom end of town an hour or so later I've had enough and want to go home. I use the loo on the way back to the car and put in a new tampon, badly. The blood doesn't seem to be enough, nor is there much pain. I almost *want* the pain, some kind of physical ache to take away from the emotional one, but it is just not there. Part of me fleetingly wonders again if I am pregnant. If I am that rare person... I suspect this is called denial.

We get to the car as the heavens open. It appears that my parents are hoping to find a tearoom on the way back to my place. I almost point out that we have just left a town full of them, but I want to go home and get warm so I stay silent. I have used up my small talk quota for the day and the reality of my situation falls back over me in its miserable little grey cloak. I stare blankly out of the window. It is getting hard to hold it all in and I want to scream.

We drive through a few towns before arriving in Rosebery: somewhere I know there to be a tearoom or two, and more interestingly a dive shop. We park. We get out and walk to the end of the village, drifting into a little place that smells distinctly of steamed fish. We sit awkwardly, squashed between a few tables. They order some coffee but I don't want anything. I can't eat or drink just to make everyone else feel more comfortable or to prove I'm okay, because I'm not okay and I can't pretend.

I say I am going to look round the shops and leave them to it. I go into the dive shop and look longingly at fins and wetsuits, before going into the pharmacy, hovering at the pregnancy tests then leaving, not entirely sure why I went in there in the first place. Eventually I find myself in a furniture shop. I really want to sit in one of the comfortable chairs and close my eyes, but no one wants a strange, withdrawn woman sitting in their armchair, ruining any possible chance of a sale, while she tries to avoid the world outside. I leave, having walked around the store as slowly as was humanly possible, and plod back out into the grey.

I see my parents by the car looking for me. I go over and get in without saying anything. Dad puts the radio on. He doesn't know what to say and my silence creates a vacuum. We get home and I put on my pyjama bottoms and dressing gown, leaving the rest of my clothes still on. I fill a hot water bottle for my frozen hands and have a glass of water. I will eat later. The carpenter might make me something if I ask nicely. I can't be bothered to do it myself. Eventually my parents leave for their hotel – we have no room at the inn for them to stay these days.

It isn't till later on that I lose the plot. I can feel it creeping over me as the evening wears on. I find myself squeezing my hands, digging my nails into my palms until it hurts. I am feeling anxious. I don't know why, but I am terribly, terribly, anxious. The carpenter is getting tired and will soon need to go to bed and I am scared of sitting up on my own. I start to knock my head on my knees. Lightly at first and then as I start enjoying the pain I really go for it. It hurts, but I *like* it. I bite great teeth tracks into my hands. The carpenter doesn't notice and so I continue, biting myself hard. When this isn't enough, I go to the kitchen and pull out a sharp little olive skewer from the middle drawer and drag it across my palm. I sense myself crossing a line and put it away.

Back in the lounge, the carpenter is still watching telly; he does nothing. He doesn't know what to do I'm sure, but this makes it worse. I need him to *help* me. The pain and the anger and the frustration are burning inside me and I feel like I am about to explode. The boiling ball of wrath in my stomach and his detachment pushes me over the edge. I grip the lounge rug, pulling it away from the floor in my white, clenched fists, banging my stupid hurt head, wanting with every thud just to drive away the stab of this loss, beat this awful pain into submission. I just want it to go away.

The stepson comes into the front room and pulls me off the floor, forcing me to stop hurting myself. I apologise over and over through my tears. He hugs me and passes me to his father. The carpenter says I must be strong, but I am tired of it all. I am *so* tired. And no one understands. Nobody sees how long I have already been strong in my life, the things I have already dealt with. And perhaps having babies was thrust upon me too soon, but still I crave it. I desperately want it and it hurts all the more for it. I don't feel like I am strong. I don't feel I can *ever* be strong again. I just feel exhausted.

There is nothing more to say, so the carpenter picks me up and puts me in bed.

11th April

It is Wednesday and I am crying into my soup. It doesn't make the soup taste bad, if anything it was under-seasoned. I just wonder when the tears will stop. When will these great waves of emotion stop crashing over me? When will I start feeling normal? I long for *normal*. I'm bloody exhausted by it all and am starting to feel just a little bit melodramatic. It must be all those awful drugs they've pumped me full of.

I'm seeing the post-IVF counsellor on Friday. It's a relief to have something planned. Perhaps she can answer my questions? I'm sure I have hundreds in my head. If only I could think of what they might be.

I wonder about the other girl again. The one I saw at the hospital, standing outside in the sunshine after her embryo transfer. The one who had her husband with her, holding her hand, looking at her with love and a sense of possibility, stroking her hair as she went through the undignified procedure, both of them wishing for the same thing. I wonder if she is somewhere out there like me, sitting on her own, crying into her unseasoned soup. Or is she celebrating with friends, them with champagne and her with lemonade, but in a champagne glass? I'll never know, of course, but I can't help but wonder. Would I like her to be sad like me, or am I jealous that I'm not happy like her?

My friends from Bangkok had the same scenario as us with their first round. They got lucky the second time, so they say I'll be fine too. My phone is going berserk. The messages are coming in thick and fast from my nearest and dearest. They say they're sorry and that I'm not to worry, it'll work better when we're more relaxed and know what to expect. The odds will be on our side this time. But that's the thing about odds and probabilities. You get the same chance each time. It *doesn't* change. The odds don't alter. You just have another go with the same odds. And what if they're wrong and I don't get lucky next time? Whose story will I find hope and comfort in then?

There are lots of people on the internet in my situation. When I'm not filling in numbers in the Sudoku book I obsess over, I'm obsessing online, looking at success stories to give me hope – which ultimately makes me cry because so many people actually *did* get lucky. Then I try the failure stories so that I can feel less alone. These just make me depressed.

> *Fingers crossed for the fifth time round, babybootiful!*
> *Sending baby dust your way!*
> *Just starting seventh cycle, wish me luck :)*
> *Anybody got any top tips for my ninth cycle? Still hoping!*

It's never-ending.

12th April

The carpenter rouses me to say goodbye, so I don't wake up to an empty bed. Today, I do feel a little different. Not better exactly, but different. My head is sore, that's for sure, but I feel a little calmer. As he leaves for work, the carpenter suggests that maybe we should move. A new start in a new house. We've been chewing this over for some time but I haven't felt like I could leave my home before, the little two-up two-down house I bought after my first marriage collapsed. I think it over some more, wondering if things have now changed for me. I am still in bed. It is 10.00am. I have nothing to get up for.

11.00am. My friend from Bangkok is calling. I am on the verge of screening the call as I am finding it so hard to talk to people. I have nothing to say. But I answer, and I am glad that I do. She is probably the most pragmatic of all my friends. She is like me in a lot of ways, almost a little too blunt, and although I do not necessarily want to hear what she is saying I know she is right. I am at rock bottom now but it will get better, come what may.

Speaking to her lifts me. Or at least kicks me into getting

out of bed to see my mum and dad, who have let themselves in with their key. I get washed. I make a little more effort than on previous days. I actually choose some clothes to put on rather than just selecting the first things that my hand falls on. I put on my new perfume. We walk down to town and I find I am quite chatty. I've thought about the moving idea and have decided it will be a good thing, so I talk about the house we will buy and what we might do with it. As we approach the main junction I see a sign for the Thursday antique fair and I know my mum will want to go in. I do not. *I* want to go to Boots to buy a multi-pack of pregnancy tests. (One to use today to make doubly, triply, quadruply sure, the rest to keep for next time.) I feel safer knowing that there will be a next time and I am getting ready and prepared for that. He has said it now. He's *promised*. I run in and buy them quickly before retracing my steps towards the antiques fair to find my parents.

Once Mum's tired herself out with the bouquet of other people's old furniture, we wander down to the Halifax, as I need to do some banking. The woman in front of me is taking an age at the cashpoint. She is talking to the machine which, alas, is not making it go any quicker. Finally she departs and I roll my eyes at her from behind my sunglasses, stepping up to the keypad. My card won't go in. I take a deep breath and try again. The machine swallows the card and promptly spits it out. It does this twice more and I am getting annoyed.

I try again, once more for luck (before I lamp it one!) when a peppy figure in a uniform comes over and asks if I need any assistance. I tell her in my best 'irritated customer' voice that their machine is playing up and won't accept my card. She takes one look at what I am trying to do and says, 'Oh no, Madam. That's your Boots Advantage Card.'

Suddenly on the edge of tears again, I mutter something

about being sorry, resisting the urge to tell her why I am totally incapable and stuff the real card in. I don't tell Mum and Dad about my card machine stupidity because they will find it funny. And it *is*. But I have had a sense of humour bypass. I can do chatty, but I can't laugh and joke. I am not ready for that yet. Perhaps when I can laugh again I'll know I'm okay.

I get a card for my grandpa for his birthday, I check Waterstones for the Zita West book about fertility I want, which they don't have, then I sit with Dad and wait while Mum gets her new phone sorted out. There are mothers everywhere. Although what did I expect? I moved my life here, post awful divorce, because it is a nice family area. Good schools, nice neighbourhoods, kiddie classes and coffee mornings. I thought that eventually, one day, I would be part of this scene, part of one of those families. Now I am not so sure. What a cruel thing, to be faced with the prospect of forever watching everyone else be a mummy, out with their kids and husbands, while I sit on the periphery.

Mum and Dad set off for home. It feels like a long wait until the carpenter will get back. I do some washing, then pull out the computer and go online. There are books to buy, houses to search for, time to kill. The stepson is home. I don't mind him living with us at all. I would never wish him away, even though it's hard for me at the moment. A constant reminder that the carpenter has, and I have not.

Then

I remember the first time I met his child, the stepson, with his quirky hairstyle and gothic black eyeliner. He was hardly a child at 14 but it was still important that we get along. We went to Brighton for the day and nervously ate chips at the end of the pier. More out of habit than anything else, I started throwing them high into the air for the seagulls to catch. The stepson, having been quite guarded to begin with, found this hilarious and we both started to relax, our nerves dissipating. And the more chips we threw, the easier it became. I think we threw more chips than we ate that day. But I was so glad he seemed to like me. I wanted his acceptance and approval because I'd decided about the carpenter and me by then.

Initially, I hadn't been sure of what I wanted and the idea of there being an 'us' had taken some time to grow on me. But it *had* grown on me. *He* had, *we* had, and so I knew I had to make it work with his son too: make an effort, forge a bond somehow. I wasn't prepared to step into his child's life on a whim, or as part of a quick fling, only to step out of it again. It would not have been fair. By the time I met the stepson, I was committed. Totally. I won't toy with people's lives or shift goalposts.

We spent some wonderful days together, the stepson and me. Once, we sold a bit of old gold that I found in the bottom of my jewellery box, some old charms and a twisty bracelet, and off we went to London for the day. He'd always wanted to go to Harrods. He's very into designer brands and fashion and we had a great time mentally spending thousands. I bought him a bottle of aftershave that he'd wanted for ages, and we had proper hot chocolate and fat cream cakes in the Parisian tearoom in the back. It was here that the stepson told me his secret, even though I'd suspected it all along. He trusted me enough to tell me he was gay. But he didn't want his father to know, not yet. He seemed relieved to have finally told someone, and I was touched that he chose me. I promised to keep his confidence as we headed off to our next stop, the London Aquarium, where we spent three full hours watching the fish butterfly through the water. He listened intently as I identified them for him, trying to explain just how beautiful it is in the world under the ocean, how it feels to hang weightless and free. I told him that one day I'd teach him to scuba dive too, just like me.

I think back to Greece, the holiday we went on as a family: the stepson, the carpenter and me. It was very hot, the roads all but deserted. We stayed in a private villa high up in the hills near a pretty little village with a funny name and an oddly shaped square. The bougainvilleas were all in bloom and their scent and vibrant colour eliminated the grey of England that seemed to hang on into the summer.

The carpenter loves the heat and spends endless hours soaking up the sun on the back patio, leaving us to our own devices. We are a good little team, the stepson and I. We spend hours chatting and walking. He is interested in life, far more than his father is, and I feel he must have a lot of his mother in him. He wants to see the world, experience *everything*. He is so desperate to be a grown-up. He asks a million interesting questions and I thrive on igniting little flames within him, fuelling him with a sense of possibility and newfound confidence. I tell him my stories, the ones that have brought me to here. He is honest and frank, mature for his age, and so, to a degree, I can be frank too.

On one of the days, we go looking for an ostrich farm mentioned in the guidebook. It's supposed to be nearby but we have been driving in circles for ages. At one point we drive down a treacherous mountain road that has a sheer drop on one side and several hairpin bends that, frankly, a mountain goat would be lucky to descend without falling to its death. Deciding it's time to ask for help we pull into a roadside café, dust flying everywhere. The stepson and I jump out and trot inside. We ask the waiter, in our best broken Greek, where we can find the ostriches. A strange expression comes over the man's face and suddenly it's as if we're in a room with Sacha Baron Cohen.

'So. You wan' to find the Giont Chickons?'

The stepson and I look at each other with giggles in our eyes before returning our straightened-out gaze to the man before us.

'Er, yes, that's right. We want to find the giant chickens,' I say slowly.

'Okay,' he says, as if we are both 007 and he is giving us our mission (should we choose to accept it). 'You go out. You go straight across the motorway. You don' go left, you don' go right, you go *straight*. You keep driving for five minutes. And then...' (dramatic pause) '... you will find the giont chickons.'

We say a twittery thank you and leave. By the time we get back to the car we are dying from laughter. The 'giont chickons' have been a mere five-minute drive away from where we started the whole time. When we finally arrive at the place we find no exciting attraction, but a single pair of ostriches in a small pen, looking at us with their ugly great eyes and doing nothing in particular. It isn't a great outing. But the getting there was fantastic!

We decide to go to the beach instead and stay till sundown. The carpenter, once again lying with his eyes closed against the sun, leaves the stepson and I to chat away. He doesn't attempt to join in much. He is pleased he doesn't have to bother with conversation, content to let us entertain each other. It is not like that for the whole holiday, sometimes he does engage with us, and we do have a terrific time. But I am aware that I'm having more fun with the stepson than with him. We have become good pals, we have accepted each other and, truthfully, he already means more to me than his father does.

Now

Sitting on the sofa, scouring the digital world for things I 'need', I realise that it is the stepson who has picked me up, a soggy, sobbing, limp little person, these last few days. *Him,* not my husband. The carpenter has done the bare minimum: nothing more, nothing less. The stepson is wonderful with his words, and his level of understanding belies his years, but I do not want to put the strain of this onto his shoulders. After all, he is very young. It is *my* burden and I want to be fair to him as I tear through my various stages of grief.

I look over to the stepson. He is brainstorming, trying to decide what he'll do with his life. He wants to get a job of some sort and start saving, maybe learn to drive, and I pass the time until the carpenter comes home by watching him work.

I think about the project the carpenter and I will have, to keep us going until we see the doctors and begin again. In times of crisis I need a project. This time it's going to be a new house. Something that is *ours,* so at least we still feel like we are moving forward in our lives *together*. At the moment we are stuck, like everything depends on us having a baby. It's too much pressure. We were considering moving anyway, and we *need* to now, as we have the stepson with us permanently. My small two-bedroomed place isn't big enough any more. That said, I love this little house and it will be a wrench to leave it. My place. But that's exactly what it is. Mine. Not ours.

I remember back to when I finally got the keys, it was

cold as hell and rained incessantly. There was a lot of work to do, a lot more than I'd originally thought. And so I busied myself in those early post-divorce days, up to my eyeballs in it. Little did I know then that my journey through DIY to independence would bring me here...

Then

I'm on my hands and knees, caked in muck. Half the floor
is missing and the rest of it is standing around me in various
collections that resemble a small timber yard. The only part
of me that is visible to anyone entering the building is my
arse. I'm having a good old look under the floorboards,
foraging around to survey the damage. The woodworm is
everywhere. Marvellous, I think to myself, who doesn't
love that sort of challenge. Not to mention the prospect
that I'll be sleeping with hundreds, if not thousands, of
horrid little bugs as they munch my home out from under
my feet... A little pre-Christmas present, if you will. The
good news is that only *some* parts of the floor have been
completely eaten through. Well, I say *good*...

Obviously I'd much rather there had been no little
beasties whatsoever and I could have gone straight ahead
with the much more exciting job of painting pretty colours
on the walls and deciding which Laura Ashley lamp and
living room curtains I'd like. Oh well, the curtains will
have to wait.

Knackered from the day's efforts, I look at the clock on
the oven, praying that it is actually correct. I discover that
it's rather later than I thought and I still haven't eaten. I'm
shattered. Shall I have a bath now or later? Is there even
any point? After all, I will probably get just as grubby
tomorrow. Perhaps I should just not wash until the whole
project is finished as some sort of experiment to see if your
body does in fact, over time, become self-cleaning. I decide
against this and put the bath on. It is the only place I can
get even remotely warm at the moment, despite running
my heating round the clock. I will have to tape up the air

vents or start wearing thermal underwear. Too much to do and it's already 8.00pm. I've decided – as my current job died a death well before Christmas, yet mercifully left me with a reasonable redundancy payout in its wake – that I'm going to be a builder-ette until January, and get my place ship-shape. I shall be wearing nothing but overalls and worker-type clothes during this time to help get me into character. My drama group would be so proud, they love a bit of method acting. And after all, it can't be that hard... Can it?

My belly squeals at me and brings me back to the moment so I decide to put the building works out of my head and cook something instead. I scratch around in the freezer for something, anything that looks vaguely appetising. I spy a pizza. That'll do, that's food, that'll be nice. I get into the bath as the pizza cooks in the oven. The dirt floats off me as I submerge myself in the water and for the first time that day, I relax. I thought the work here would be easy. Well, easy-ish. Certainly do-able! You know, rip a carpet out here, destroy a cupboard there... Tart it up a bit, paint some walls, change a few fixtures, maybe gut the horrid little bathroom and install a decent one. I did not envisage having to replace whole sections of floor – or the horrors I would find under them.

The first thing I'd done on arrival was rip out the foam-backed scrag of a carpet from the main bedroom. It was a delightful forest green colour, and smelled of old mildew and baby sick. It was dragged out into the rain before I'd even taken a box from the removal truck. Not that there was actually much to unpack. Aside from my personal things, clothes, DVDs and the like, I'd only come away from my first marriage with some basic kitchenware, a rug, a wardrobe, an ironing board and a Dyson. The ex-husband had been particularly miffed to lose the Dyson, I recall.

My aunt had donated a bed and I set myself up in the back bedroom, camping out as I got to work. For some reason there were two windows between that bedroom and the lounge – who the hell knows why – so I decided these were coming out and getting bricked in. I took the lump hammer to them, using every bit of strength I had (and a bit more besides) and dragged them to the car, the weight of them doing the poor thing no favours whatsoever. I'm fairly sure I did some irreparable damage to the suspension as I drove to the tip and dumped them, all the while praying that I hadn't killed my beloved VW.

Over the next few days, I got a man or two in to quote for the plumbing and plastering. Both quotes were ridiculously high. One chap wanted £2,000 for a day's worth of plumbing. Perhaps he was some sort of celebrity plumber, or the radiators were made of gold, but either way he wasn't getting the job. In the end, my dad said he would come down on the weekends to help out. A few days later I turned 30.

I reluctantly emerge from the bath. I'm finally warm, having been in for nearly half an hour with just my eyes and nose poking out of the water like a hippo. The pizza is done. I am ravenous and my mind drifts about, reminding me that I still have a lot to plan and a long way to go.

Christmas comes and goes, as do the bug men, who are quite nice to watch, naked from the waist up, as they work. I stay away for a couple of days at the non-boyfriend's once they've finished so I don't die from the fumes and a week later my mum and dad come down to help me rebuild the necessary sections of my floor.

I get up in the mornings and put my work clothes straight over my pyjamas. There is little point in changing or showering, as the dust and dirt are everywhere. I am quite enjoying learning how to do all this. I am ditching the last of my baggage and rebuilding myself. I even tackle the huge job of sanding the floors by myself. I check out a million different websites to establish how one might achieve it without having to scour the varnish off by hand, and also to see how horribly expensive it might be to get 'the boys' in to do it for me. There is a plethora of online demonstrations, all showing the latest techniques for getting the floor of your dreams and, do you know what, they actually make it look rather easy. Who needs the boys? This looks like fun! It will be easy...

Not so easy in fact. I hire a sander, but by the time I have loaded the sandpaper I'm knackered. This does not bode well, and I begin to think that the job may be considerably more difficult than the video suggested. I plug in the sander and the beast lurches to life, dragging me across the living room, chewing a great crater out of the floor as it goes. I turn it off at the wall, terrified, and stare at it for a long moment as if it has done it on purpose. Shaking a little, I try again. It kicks back into gear, throwing itself forward, munching the floor that stands in its path. It is literally mowing the top of my floorboards off, with me chasing it around getting very upset by the whole affair. Two hours later, I've had all I can stand. I'm shaking from the effort and I flop down, half-choking amid sawdust and ends of heavy-duty sandpaper to survey the scene. It is utter chaos. There are now great lanes across the floor and it's rather rough in places. I will have to refine these as, despite their rustic charm, they may take the underside of someone's foot off. The job has defeated me completely. The sander didn't get past its first whir before hurling itself across the floor, with me still attached to it. I decide that I'll simply return it to the shop and be grateful it didn't kill me.

My parents stay for a few days. We go to the builders'

merchants to get some supplies for the plumbing, and halfway round the shop we remember I'll need a load of carpentry doing too. Mum steps up to the counter and asks the assistant if he knows a man who can. The man behind the counter pauses and shouts though a door behind him: 'Who does the most carpentry?' I do not quite hear the name they shout back but I take a piece of paper with a number on it. We get back to mine and have a brew before my mum and dad get off home. Then I dial the number.

When I open the door to him at 8.00pm that evening I am still in my dusty work clothes with half the house in my hair. He is tall and stocky with wayward curls, two-day-old stubble and a red nose from the cold. He's wearing a dustman's hat and a quirky, amused smile.

I have a mental flashback to the lady with the black cat. *'You're going to get a proposal.'* And it isn't like angels descend in a heavenly choir, there is no epiphany, no harp music, but somehow I know it is going to be him. He is going to be the one who proposes. And I have no idea how we get to there from here, but I know it is going to be him.

And all I can say is, 'Hello, you must be the carpenter.'

Now

I wake up with a start to find that I've fallen asleep on the couch. It's around 4.00pm now and the carpenter will be home soon. The stepson has disappeared into his room. I start to search the internet. I want something to show for my day. I want to find us a house, to unearth the project that will give us focus and direction. We desperately need something that is *ours*. And it will help to pass the time too, work out the heartache, and give us something tangible to plough it all into. Something more concrete than hope.

I ring the hospital. They didn't call me back to arrange a follow-up appointment as they'd promised and the lack of this small piece of structure has ruffled me. I need *definites* right now. So I call them. I take charge of it.

But the news isn't welcome. We have to wait for three months before we can have another round. Three! They can't even give me exact dates as it depends on what my body does. It has to recover, they say, it is a hard process. No kidding. What do they know about it anyway? They don't have to go through it. They don't get that one of the hardest parts is right now: the waiting, the not knowing, and the desperate need to try again. I thought it would be just a few weeks. I've busied myself all day with nothing, how much more nothing can I do?

I'm glad I'm seeing the counsellor tomorrow. It is 'free', a part of the package, and I seem to be borderline loopy so why not? But then what? After that? Perhaps I should try to book that trip to Paris we've been talking about for the last three years? Break up the time with a holiday? I quickly look at Paris breaks on lastminute.com. The prices aren't too horrific, so when he gets home, I hit him with my idea straight away. He's not keen. Lots to do, lots to pay for, lots to save for, he says. And although I know he's right I feel deflated. I need a rest and a break and I'm sad that we can't go, even for just a night. But I don't have my own money any more. That ended when I left work to have this treatment.

He goes into the kitchen and makes a sandwich without offering me one. We watch TV. He cracks open a bottle of wine. I try not to notice.

13th April

It is Friday 13th: an ominous date for some, but I have embraced it. After all, things can't get *much* worse. And I find I've had a bit of a breakthrough. Today I made some logical sense of how I've been feeling. Well, the counsellor at the hospital did. She explained why I feel like I do. Why I like the idea of getting into the water, why the thought of it is appealing and safe. It is not about death. I do not want to kill myself.

That was a relief. I didn't *think* I did. I'm glad I'm not insane. But I *am* in a fragile place.

The counsellor said that I crave getting into the water because when I'm in there, there is no one else. I can shut the world out. It is a place where there is *only* me, with no one else's lives, thoughts, stresses or dramas to weigh me down or overshadow everything that *I* might want or be feeling. She said it simply. She took what I'd said about my life and relationships and summed it all up in about two sentences. I like it that she simplified the mess in my head. It makes it feel less...well, messy really.

I told her about the other night, when I lost it. I told her everything, in glorious Technicolor. I was embarrassed and worried. Was I heading for a nervous breakdown? She said that it was a cry for help, that I was ready to burst because I needed to be listened to, heard, especially by *him*. I wanted him to understand and alter his behaviour towards me.

A lot of the time I listen to everyone else. I help others with their emotions and crises. Some people listen in return, they help and they are there for me too, but a lot of people don't. They just keep taking what they need from me, until there is nothing left of me for me. And they do it with little regard for my well being. *He* is one of them, she says – my carpenter, my husband. I've tried to be selfless but it's been to my detriment. I've almost robbed myself of the chance to know what *I* want from my relationships. I know what everybody else wants and expects from me, but do I know what I want for myself?

I've been told all my life to be strong, to just keep going and not allow things to get me down. Stiff upper lip, get yourself up, dust yourself off and start all over again: it has made me tough. But what I want now is to be heard. To have someone say, 'There, there, it's okay.' To help me to rationalise my feelings and talk about them openly and honestly, not push them down inside, force them away and keep plodding endlessly on.

Since my first marriage ended, I have never really felt like there has been time for me to stop: to sit, to reflect, to simply feel how I feel. I've craved it. I suddenly see the value in counselling.

The carpenter does not see it. I've been asking him to see someone to help with his past and his drinking, but he refuses to acknowledge that there is a problem. I'm not entirely sure why it is that he drinks, what the cause of his deep-seated unhappiness is, but I wish he would address it, that he'd *choose* to, for all our sakes. It has always been a problem, his need to reach for the red. The stepson told me about the times he saw his dad unconscious, lolling around the floor with his eyes rolling around in his head. Once, they couldn't rouse him at all. He thought his dad was dead. He was eleven at the time.

At the beginning of our relationship the problem wasn't so obvious. At first, I just thought he was a fast drinker. If I didn't keep up with him he would guzzle my share of the wine too, so I tried to keep pace with him for a time. It wasn't long before I realised that he 'liked' a drink. We were going through a lot of wine each week and I started to get chubby on it, soft rolls appearing around my back and waistline. I felt bloated and blobby, and when I brought it up he reined himself in swiftly. But he didn't stay reined in for long. He can easily go through a bottle as he sits and watches the roast cook. (Why he needs to actually sit and *watch* it, I don't know. Maybe he is waiting for some sort of basting emergency?)

These days he can easily drink two full bottles to himself. I can't take him to functions any more, through fear that he'll have one too many and say embarrassing things. So I've tried getting him to go seek help. But it hasn't worked and, because the problem is just about manageable, or so I tell myself, I haven't pushed it with him. He thinks the idea of counselling is pathetic. It makes me feel pretty rubbish, as this must be what he thinks of me.

That said, I was a cold fish at my appointment with the counsellor. Well, it was either that or be a crying wreck and somehow I just couldn't let myself cry in there. One day I hope I will feel that I don't have to be strong all the time. Maybe then I won't need to sit opposite a stranger to enjoy being heard? Maybe one day *the carpenter* will listen. I want so much for him to see that my feelings are valid, as are the things that I would like for myself. I am not being selfish, I want what I always said I did. My goals remain unchanged.

14th April

The counsellor *has* helped. I feel different today. Not better, as in fully recovered or healed, just different.

I have a job offer from that marketing company and the idea of it helps pull me back into the real world. It offers some definition to the time stretching before me. I feel easier. I don't feel the need to get into the water. I *will* get in the shower and wash my hair though! At the moment I resemble a matted Afghan Hound.

I'm singing in a fundraising concert tomorrow with my drama group. It's been in the diary for months and months and I'd all but forgotten about it. They phoned this morning to make sure I still want to do it, as I've been absent from rehearsals. These last few days and weeks have totally absorbed me, the time passing strangely and slowly. It will be good to be useful, so I've said I'll go and sing.

Another little event is that I had my first glasses of wine since the treatment cycle. It felt so nice to be normal. But that's my limit now: two glasses. The carpenter has promised to stick to the same but I wonder if he will. I have to try to trust him, and not badger him. They say you must work up to your treatment cycles, be super-good in the months before it: limited drinking, folic acid, good healthy food all round and *no stress*. The last one I fear may be easier said than done.

I try to pick out clothes for the concert. The little silk dress from Warehouse maybe, with the shoes from Dune that I bought a year ago and have never worn? I do that with shoes sometimes, buy them and never wear them. I buy them because they are tiny and pretty and I am a shoe magpie. Then I realise that they are totally impractical, I can't walk in them and just keep them in my wardrobe – in their box of course – getting them out occasionally to admire. How messed up is that? Maybe I *am* a nutter? Someone cool once told me they were cool, so I decide to trust her. I will *wear the shoes*.

I'm not sure I'm cool any more. That said, I'm not entirely sure I ever was. As a teenager I was guilty of wearing a cotton Lycra all-in-one with a blue silk shirt over the top tied at the waist. I also had a silk jacket with shoulder pads, usually worn over a crop top and denim shorts. These days I like simple lines and tops from Next. Perhaps I have bypassed cool and gone straight from tragic to middle aged? Perhaps fashion is subjective anyway. Either way, I really must endeavour to wear all my shoes.

I pack my bag carefully: dress, tights, shoes, make-up, music and my lucky bear, making sure that nothing is forgotten. I settle into bed to do some Sudoku and look over my words for tomorrow. And for the first time since the morning after, I feel I am breathing with my own lungs again. The weight on my chest has lifted.

15th April

The fundraiser is an interesting affair. We've teamed up with a few other groups and hired a venue hidden away behind Leicester Square. It's exciting to be somewhere other than our local theatre, though no one really knows who's in charge and it's all a bit disorganised – with some very dubious performances from a local college who swan around backstage as if they've made it to the West End. One person thought it would be a good idea to put a silver curtain around the keyboard so it looked, and I quote, 'snazzy'. It doesn't look snazzy, it looks tacky, like something from the pier in Blackpool.

We do our usual set, which goes without a hitch, and I sing well. I feel better for it, more like my old self. It is wonderful to see my friends too. They tell me that it'll all be all right in the end. We hang around chatting afterwards and I spot a familiar face in the crowd. My favourite work friend is here with her husband. I go over to her, really quite excited as I've not seen her in ages, but as she turns to me I notice straight away. She is sporting a bump. My face falls a little – I had no idea she was pregnant – but I recover quickly and realise I am genuinely pleased for her. I don't get that all-too-familiar sinking feeling. Then she says that she hadn't told me because she didn't want to upset me. She means to be kind but I feel hideous that she felt she couldn't tell me. My plight has affected her too, paused our friendship.

The carpenter isn't here to see me faced with her bump, he hasn't come to watch. He rarely does any more. He takes a lot less interest than he did in the early days, when the fact that I performed was still exciting. I think back to the opening night of the first show he came to, three years ago...

He was keyed up, *I* was feeling bland and nervy. My face had been painted into place, my slightly-too-short hair sculpted into an up-do of sorts and I was acutely aware that I was *very* nervous. Not because I had to perform, no, because the *carpenter* had never seen me perform before. That was way more scary than performing to 300 people I'd never met – I desperately wanted him to see that I was good, even though I only had a few solo lines. I sat twiddling my fingers, ready far too early, winding myself up beautifully. But two hours later, and with only a couple of marginal costume disasters, I was out of the woods, knackered and sweaty but thoroughly relieved. The local rag would be thrilled and the coffers filled for next year's production. After much jostling and darting semi-naked past the boys, I de-sweated and was at the stage door, the wind filling my tired lungs and drying out my hair. And he was there waiting for me, grinning with pride. And I loved him more, because he *got* it. He saw who I was in this world that he didn't really understand. He saw what it all meant to me and why I did it. He pulled me into him and kissed me. He thought I was good and that was all that mattered.

We all went for a drink and he let me do the rounds, chatting with the locals. He was proud. He waited patiently and, when I was ready, we headed home, stopping at a kitsch little bar on the way for another drink. When we got back, there was that smile, his 'I've got a secret' smile. And then I saw them sitting in a vase, a pretty bunch of yellow roses.

'I didn't know if I was meant to take them to the theatre or not,' he said. 'They're for you, for tonight...'

I can almost smell those lovely roses as I come back to my friend and her bump. We talk a little more before I hug her goodbye, promising to see her soon. For a while I look at the spot where she was standing, knowing that I am being left behind. It doesn't upset me exactly, I just feel a bit lost. It is a week today since it all went wrong. I really can't believe it. Only a week, yet it seems like forever. I feel like asking for a refund. I remember myself at the start of the IVF. I'd been quite pragmatic about it all then. Or, at least, I put great efforts into making an outward show of coping...

Then

I am forcing myself to be calm. It's as if I am looking up at Mount Kilimanjaro, knowing that I have to get to the top where the air is thin, way above the clouds. I've been packed off with a rucksack of goodies: my kit, my needles and drugs, and he's wished me luck and said he'll be there for me. It's going to be a long climb but I'm sure I can do it if I just go one mile at a time, steady and resolute. I am happy to finally be on my way.

As for staying relaxed, I've bought a CD to achieve this: 'Belief, Bump, Baby! Hypnotise your way through your treatment cycle.' Last night, I actually fell fully asleep and woke up part way through the second track on the disc. I hope I haven't asked my body to do two things at once? At least I was *genuinely* relaxed.

You'd think that when you get to this point in life that it would be an exhilarating time. For years you've dreaded the double line on the pregnancy test, now you pray for it. You picture lots of romantic nights in with your partner, candles in the bedroom, moving together in harmony as you create life with a thousand little love bubbles floating around you. The reality of our situation couldn't be more different. It is definitely not romantic. But I'm trying my best to accept things for what they are and invest fully in this way of doing it.

I'm trying to keep my mind busy with other things too so I don't obsess, doing lots of odds and sods around the house while I still feel up to it. They say that the further into the treatment you get, the more you start to feel as if you've been sat on by a horse, so today I'm taking advantage of feeling fine. I cleared out the shed, mended a chair, sanded and painted two others, blacked the fireplace, tidied out my toolbox, threw out some useless and broken things, along with those that I didn't know the purpose of...

I probably should have spread it out a bit. To the average person I've probably just described an entire year's worth of DIY. But I'm not used to having all this time to myself.

It was a hard decision to go on sabbatical from the crazy busy job that I loved. I'd been there since just after I met the carpenter. I'd scouted around for weeks, trying to find something as I slowly ran out of money, getting nowhere. But, just as I was panicking that I might have to string my last tin of beans out for a month to afford my new mortgage, a guy from my old office phoned. We were both interns years ago, working for an entrepreneurial type who produced theatre and radio. He told me that a big agent he knew was looking for a very hands-on assistant. I barely let the line go dead before I called them to apply for the job – and a few weeks later, I started work in their classy offices on the Strand in central London.

The hours were nuts even then. Theatre most nights, drinks, events to organise, clients to manage. I loved it. They've been so generous in giving me this time off while I go through the treatment cycle. They don't want someone dipping in and out, or being a hormonal wreck, so they're happy, for now, to get someone else in... My only concern is that if this doesn't work, will they be so understanding a second or third time around?

Still, I'm quite glad not to be worrying about work, in a way. The novelty of only having to cook for my husband, run errands and watch *Coronation Street* still holds a certain amount of marital excitement.

The downregulation drugs I'm on are hard work. They make your ovaries and uterus completely flatline, pushing your hormones down until there is no activity from them whatsoever. They make me feel strange and hollow. I get hot flashes and wonder if this is what it feels like to be menopausal.

So far I've had mixed success at administering them. It really isn't easy. The needles are those big hypodermic affairs and I handle the plunger with shaky hands and the refined skill of a gloved boxer. I've managed to give myself a belly full of bruises, which is not very attractive at all. I do look quite heroin chic, though it's a lot more 'addict' than 'model'...

I have decided that, since all this soreness, I am no longer prepared to jab myself in the belly as advised. I am going into my waist fat instead – I knew I'd find a use for it eventually. And I will also be pre-icing my skin.

I'm keeping myself positive and happy about things as much as I can. I don't want to let the stress and anxiety of the run-up to this milestone invade the actual, important matter of carrying it all out, even though it's been a thorny time for us. I'm sure that once we get to the difficult bit, the carpenter will be back on board – buoying me up, keeping me going, happy that we are doing this.

Now

Going home on the late bus, I think back over the very beginning, before we'd even begun dating. I turn it over and over in my mind, replaying certain scenes again and again, wondering if I should have made different choices. I remember how very unsure I'd been – despite what the lady with the black cat had predicted, or maybe because of it? – but I still somehow ended up dating him. I remember his persistence, how he'd chased...

The bus clunks to a halt outside my house and I tiptoe inside so as not to wake him. I know he has to get up frightfully early. I clamber into bed, thinking of my friend's bump and wonder if I'll get my own soon. I'm the only one out of our group who isn't in the 'mummy club' now and a lot of the time I feel very isolated because of it.

He stirs as I slip under the covers beside him but he carries on sleeping, his hand resting on the pillow by my face. I look at his hands a lot while he sleeps – he doesn't know I do this. I feel them as I lie there in the half darkness as he sleeps off a hard day's graft and run my fingers through his, circling the lumps and bumps and the creases that resemble canyons, finding strange comfort in how well I know *them* at least. They don't elude me like he does at times. They remind me of how hard he works. Real work. Not sitting at a desk doing mentally tiring stuff like a lot of us do, but real, honest, good old-fashioned, sweating-your-arse-off work.

He has strange knuckles on one of his hands, the right one. He's a righty, I'm a lefty. He has distinctive calluses across his thumbs, especially the one he uses to hold his chisel. The callus is hard and has sort of contracted over time. He stirs again, so I leave him to his dreams and turn over to try to remember mine.

Then

The carpenter is coming back to drop the key off later this evening. He's been working here all day while I've been out. Why did I agree to this? I'm sure it's a flimsy excuse to see me out of hours. Why didn't I just make him leave the key after he finished, have him post it through the letterbox or something? It's not that he isn't nice, it's just that I'm tired and I want nothing more than to have a bath and go to bed.

'Oh well,' I mutter. 'Nothing much to be done about it now.'

And after all you did agree to this, chips in my subconscious. *Quite happily, I might add!*

I choose to ignore my annoying inner radio in favour of the *actual* radio while I wash up, but it's not long before it kicks back in, drowning out yet another rendition of 'Love Lifts Us Up Where We Belong' on Magic FM.

He is nice to you. He's pretty handsome. And he's good with his hands! Everyone else thinks you should give him a chance.

I turn the real radio off and get stroppy with myself at this point. 'Yes, look, all right, he's really sweet, very nice and all that but I'm really not looking for anything at the moment. I've got quite enough on my plate with the non-boyfriend. I'm just not interested.'

Well, if you're sure...

'I am sure! Now shut up and go away, I heard the door go.'

The carpenter has let himself in (I'm not sure whether to be annoyed about this or not) and his head is poking in between the French doors, checking it's okay to come through. I immediately notice he is wearing non-work-like clothes. He looks entirely different without the crusty coatings of wood shavings and dirt...

Although if you're being honest, you do quite like the dirt and have in fact had a very strange dream where he is wearing nothing but *the dirt...*

Anyway, back to the moment. He is sporting a distinctly I'm-going-out-on-a-date type leather jacket. One which, unfortunately for him, reminds me of one Dad used to wear to the pub in the nineties. I now panic. I thought he was just going to drop the key off, possibly ask for some money and go. I was not anticipating having to entertain! I look like hell. And the house looks like, well, a building site.

He's smiling, waiting for me to say something.

'Erm... would you, er, like a... cup of tea?' I ask. (Good, a cup of tea, that's harmless enough. Good suggestion.)

I make the tea ultra-quickly and walk through to the living room to try to find somewhere to sit down with it. Surveying the scene, I realise that this could prove rather tricky. I can't see anywhere that isn't covered in dust or isn't the floor. There are tools littering the place and some level of destruction, construction or general chaos in every corner. I look sideways at the small bedroom that I've moved back into, once more the only inhabitable space, my eyes falling on the little single bed. It is the *only* possible place to sit down. It is also the only place that is *completely* inappropriate and inviting him in there will *absolutely* give him the wrong idea. I stand there for a very uncomfortable minute or so, quietly flapping. Not easy to do when trying not to spill tea.

'Shall we go to the pub?' I suggest. (Great! *Much* better. Now he *definitely* thinks he's on a date! Though it's probably preferable to my other option of: 'Why don't you come and sit here beside me on my lovely dusty bed?')

I look for non-work clothes. *Any* clothes will do – all they need to be is clean and to hand – but I'm struggling. I rummage around and throw on what I unearth. I do *not* look good. Why have I chosen to keep, for years, a polo neck (circa 1997) in fuchsia pink with uneven ribbing and overly long arms? And why it is the *only* thing I can lay my grubby hands on? Never mind. At least I am now wearing something other than decorating clothes – although I rather fancy that the fate of the fuchsia polo neck is about to change.

We head out and walk down the road to my new local, The King's Arms. It's a charming place, newly refurbished, with a cosy, snug feel to it. There are even comfy seats and a log burner, and I love it from my first step over the threshold. Perhaps this will have to act as my living room for a while? It has a sofa for a start, and that's more then I've got right now.

The carpenter goes to the bar. I make beeline for the fireplace and, for the first time in weeks, sitting down is bliss! I sink into the inexpensive foam, suddenly thankful that the carpenter came by and that we ended up coming out for drinks. As I relax, so does my mind. The carpenter catches my eye, smiling his slightly crooked smile, and my mind flicks back to a daydream of half-naked workmen, busy sweating and toiling at my beck and call...

Just as I'm getting into it, the carpenter materialises on the sofa next to me and presents me with a white wine spritzer. Quite convinced that he can read my thoughts, I feel my face start to burn up and turn a colour that nicely matches my polo neck. (This happens to me a lot. I wish I had an off-switch for it because it can strike at any moment. *The Face*. I don't have to be *really* embarrassed, but the more I realise I'm turning pink, the more I look like I am about to self-combust – and the deeper the shade of crimson I go.)

We sit and chat. The carpenter is fairly easy to talk to, surprisingly. He seems very normal. Normal is nice. Normal is *good*. It is a refreshing change for me, with regards to male company, as I'm used to more temperamental artsy types, who are (in my experience) very high maintenance! He is driving, so he's only drinking lemonade, which I'm quietly impressed by. He doesn't even have a half and I am glad that he is responsible. I allow myself to relax a touch more.

He doesn't have a *huge* amount to say for himself, but he does ask a lot of questions about me, really taking an interest. He asks what I do for a living. I say I'm between things right now but that I'm a PA and go on to tell him all about the industries I've worked in and would *like* to work in. He is making a lot of effort to get to know me and the attention is lovely, disarming. He isn't self absorbed or self-centred, he is actually interested in *me*. I tell him that I am a member of a local drama group and how much I love this. He says he'll come and watch me in the next thing we do.

It's a total change for me since I moved out here and it's nice to feel I know someone. I talk about my divorce a little bit, how I've never had children. This is something I'm both happy and sad about at the same time. I'm glad that I didn't have any in a way, because it would have been much more difficult ending my unhappy marriage if there had been children involved. But when I see my friends with their children, I see the joy that they bring (tantrums aside) and wish I had that for myself. Perhaps a baby would have cemented my marriage somehow? I say, then decide this is a ridiculous sentiment. I sound like one of those people on Jeremy Kyle, who everyone sitting at home shouts at. The ones who think that having a baby will save a failing relationship.

The carpenter listens intently as I blather on. I'm aware

that I'm hogging the conversation, though he doesn't seem too worried or bothered about adding anything much. I ask him to tell me about himself. He tells me that his own marriage, which lasted for four years, ending 11 years ago, and about his son who is now 14. I ask how old *he* is – it's very hard to judge! – and he tells me he is 40. He doesn't look it.

Eventually we seem to have talked ourselves out, for now at least, and the conversation falls quiet. I'm horrendously tired and in real danger of having to be carried to my front door, so I suggest we call it a night.

We walk back to where he has parked his funny little car, but things suddenly feel a bit awkward. I'm not sure what I'm supposed to do now. We've had a nice evening but I don't want to kiss him, and I hope he doesn't try to kiss me. It feels like he might, so I say goodnight, keeping my hands in my pockets. Once he gets a safe distance away, I surprise myself by blowing him a quick kiss – sort of out of politeness (because I feel like something more than words is expected of me here) but also sort of because I want to. A part of me *is* interested in him, though I am by no means certain in what way. He intrigues me, I think. Perhaps I'm more intrigued than interested? It's very hard to say.

I wake up late. The carpenter has gone already and the stepson is at a friend's house. I have time to myself. Space. Air. I can breathe today.

I take a hot bath. This is something else I haven't been able to do for a while, and is one of the things I have missed the most. Hot baths were on the 'forbidden list', another little piece of life that the IVF had taken away from me. But today, I can soak in the blissful heat. Some of the tension melts away into the steam and balm as I settle myself in my favoured hippo position.

It's while I'm lying here, hippo-like, that I notice just how dirty the bathroom has become. I'm a little shocked! I look around, taking in the spot-mould that is starting to form on the ceiling, and wonder if I'm really the only one who notices these things? I feel a little purpose build inside me at the prospect of tackling it, something that has escaped me these last weeks. Chemical cleaners have also been a no-no during the treatment as well, though I had sort of hoped the carpenter might have done the cleaning for me. After all, he does live here too. Why does he not help out more? Why could he not have pulled his finger out and just done a bit for me? Why is it *always* down to me?

It's strange, but I know I am starting to feel properly better now that I want to clean again. I *love* to clean. Perhaps cleaning is a part of the process, one of the stages of grief you go through? Or maybe that's just me! Up until now I haven't been able to so much as look at a duster, let alone lift one, but today I want to.

I get out of the bath, dry off and throw on some suitable clothes. Then, 'Mould & Mildew' in hand, I get to work blasting the room – bleaching, spraying, scuffing and buffing. It is as if I'm trying to polish away the past week, shining up my life again until it looks clean and gleaming once more. Well, at least to the naked eye.

I am surprised at how quickly I have ripped through all my emotions. Through grief and tears and raging hormones to cleaning and thinking ahead.

I do the rest of the house, then pull out the computer. I feel a sudden sense of urgency. It's time to move on.

The carpenter and I have both been searching for houses intermittently, though not terribly seriously. We've found about a dozen possibilities, but managed to see enough flaws in each to not bother with an actual viewing. The one that the carpenter *really* likes the look of, I've been dismissing completely, pretty much because it's ugly and has pebble dashing. Today I remind myself that one should look beneath exteriors.

I click on findaproperty.com and it's still there, unsold. Perhaps it's meant to be? With newfound purpose, and a touch of impetuousness, I pick up the phone.

'Hello. I'd like to make an appointment to view the house on Sea View Way.'

PART TWO
Making Dates

Now

15th May

Take two.

I am less nervous when I go to the hospital this time. I know the drill and I know the nurses. Any rough edges I presented in our first meetings have been smoothed as they got to know me. I feel safe in their company. They know how the carpenter can be with me. They've seen it in some things and deduced it from others. They know why I've been terse and irritable at times, and have even allowed us to skip ahead and not wait the full three months before we get going again. I am grateful for this, as I've been struggling with the thought of waiting.

I can tell they feel sorry for me because of last time, though they are not allowed to say it, and they make special efforts to put me at my ease. Like me, they appreciate just how important this all is, how make or break it could be. I don't want it to be true, but it is. There are still two little voices scratching at the inside of my head. There's the one that believes it is all entirely possible: me, him, the marriage, the baby – and then there's that other voice...

Everything is riding on this. He doesn't know it and I don't quite want to believe it, but it *is* true and it wears me down so much. But I think the loss of last time has, at least, kicked him up the behind a little. He seems to be more on board, though it never feels 100% safe or certain. Perhaps it never will be? It always seems like he's on a knife edge.

I've been liaising with the hospital for days, weeks, now about the next treatment cycle. I want to pin the dates down because I'm terrified that if there's nothing concrete he might start changing his mind, like last time. I don't want to have to go through that embarrassment again.

During the first round of treatment, I played down his attitude. I made out he was just tired, pushed myself into believing that he'd go back to the way he'd been in the very beginning, on the night in the nice pub with the cheap sofa and the expensive log burner: kind, interested and steady. If I could only get us through *this* bit, I thought, then he'd come back to me. My carpenter with the big rugged hands, who *did* grow on me and I *did* find myself loving.

He behaves as if all this is something I've asked him to do for me, but it was always the ultimate plan. It was *his* suggestion, one of the first things that came out of his mouth – little did I know that his offer came with an expiry date. He said he wanted a family. If you want a family, you *want a family*. When did it come with hidden terms and conditions? How can someone change their mind about something so fundamental? It hurt me. I felt rejected. I still do.

I sometimes think he only said it to get me to go out with him. I mean, he renewed the wrong doorframe in my house 'accidentally on purpose', then said he'd not charge me for it if I went out for dinner with him! I didn't feel I could decline so I ended up on the date. I looked past his imperfections and went along with it. I gave him a chance, to see if I could like him – to see if the lady with the long black hair had been right. To see if this was *fate*.

How did we get to the point where I've been under needle and knife if he doesn't even want it? Should we have already walked away? Should *he* have? If he didn't want kids then he should never have said he did. Surely, with his age and experience of fatherhood, he knew all along how he really felt? He engineered this. And he is now stuck with the reality of those decisions.

He didn't show any interest in that first cycle, there was no encouragement. He didn't care that I was scared of needles and was white as a sheet every time I injected, sitting up alone in bed, being 'positive' and forcing myself into a happy little world, blind (or delusional) as to the state of things. The fairies and I were busy being Zen, while he found any possible reason he could to not be there.

He said that since it was all for me, not for him, I'd have to look after the baby by myself as he didn't want – and I quote – to 'get involved' with it. What does that even mean? What kind of attitude is that? What kind of person does that make him? Not a very attractive one for a start.

If this was something I had suddenly sprung on him I could understand it. He is a bit older, he has done it all before. But *he* volunteered for this part, no one made him say he wanted it. *He* is the reason we're doing this all right now, rather than waiting. I wasn't really ready to have children yet, but I made that massive compromise for him.

The carpenter barely looked at me during the first appointment. He jabbed at the paper with his signature, practically throwing the paperwork back across the table at the startled nurse. It showed the gaping hole in our relationship. It showed I wasn't loved properly. I was actually fearful they'd say: 'You two aren't fit. You're not in a stable enough place to do this. You can't have a child through us' – and then it would be over. I was so embarrassed by him that day, I even apologised to the nurse on his behalf. That's when they started feeling sorry for me.

Despite all of that I stayed with him. I held myself together. I was hopeful and I believed. Friends called and offered their ears and it helped. It wasn't the support I truly craved but it was there for me nonetheless – though I do hate being that girl that everyone feels sorry for!

So, I'm keen to get on with this. I *need* to get on with it. My period finally came today, rather overdue. You have to wait until you get your period before they can work out your treatment dates. It is all planned to the letter, months ahead of time.

I leave the hospital with my little flow chart of the running order, a bag of hypodermic needles and my downregulation drugs. I flop into the car, setting my kit on the empty seat beside me – that shouldn't, of course, be empty of my husband – and turn the key.

As I pull away from the hospital car park, my mind is busy thinking over everything that we've got to get done. I decide that my period arriving late is not necessarily a bad thing. It buys us time. Perhaps it'll be better for the treatment to kick off a bit later. We will be in the new house by then...

We chose the house very quickly in the end. It was the one on Sea View Way. Yes, it was ugly on the outside, but when I went in, and saw its dreadful décor and just how much in need of a revamp it was, a little old flame reignited inside me. I remembered how much I love renovating, especially alongside the carpenter. Perhaps working together again will help us to rediscover what we had. Perhaps it will somehow carry us back to the beginning...

Then

He walks in, casually, magically, just in time for the tea I'm about to make, as if he knew. Builders work on a brew, maybe he has a radar?

'Just dropping by, babes,' he says.

Why does he always call me babes? Why does he always 'just drop by' unannounced? Why does he always drop by when I look like a *haystack*? I doubt he even knows what colour my hair is, as it's always so caked in building debris.

Perhaps he is checking up on me to make sure I haven't actually killed myself with my new SDS drill. (Alas, having solved the floor problem, I discovered I had damp wall problems too.) It is an enormous bloody great thing and looks like a cross between a pneumatic drill and a splurge gun from *Bugsy Malone*. Yesterday, the carpenter and I had laughed about the look on the BT engineer's face when he saw it. I was haphazardly taking chunks out of the wet wall when the man turned up to put the phoneline in. The engineer came through the door brandishing a long, thin tool with a look that said *hey, look how big my drill is!* only to be met with mine. We faced each other off for a moment, drills drawn and ready. He smiled weakly – embarrassed and outranked by my monster – and went back outside to sort out some wiring. I smiled, pulled my pink earmuff ear-defenders back into place and started her up again...

The carpenter takes his coat off and goes through to make the tea, never one to wait to be invited, which both exasperates and pleases me at the same time. Maybe he's not here checking my work, maybe he's checking me out? I don't mind. He is slowly becoming a part of my life.

Someone I notice the absence of. It's probably because I don't really know anyone else around here and I'm enjoying the familiarity of him, along with having all the help I can get.

I tell him I have to finish off the sanding in the lounge. Annoyingly this will require hiring *another* sanding machine. I am not exactly palpitating with joy at the prospect of this as I'm still rather surprised that I came out of the last attempt alive. Best not to tempt fate or push my luck. I tell the carpenter the whole sanding story, which he finds terribly funny. The image of me chasing a great roaring beast around my living room, wearing work clothes over pyjamas in pink earmuffs to deaden the din, must be rather hilarious. In great detail, I explain to him what I am looking for in this new sander. Small, efficient, not massively powerful... in a word: girly! He tells me I need a handheld one, which sounds more manageable, and promises to hire it on his account. I can pay him back, he says, though I suspect he won't actually let me do this.

The next day he drops by smiling, gallant as a knight, the proud provider of new sanding device that I'm thrilled with. We have a couple of cuppas and segue nicely into discussing the rest of the flooring.

The following week he comes over (on a Sunday no less) to lay a little laminate section in the entrance hall. This is definitely not something I want to tackle myself. If I get it wrong I'm stuffed. It is not like demolition. I am *very* good at demolition. Bashing out the fireplace, working my poor little arms till they almost fell off, to reveal a large person-sized hole (I know this because I got in it) was immensely rewarding (and toning) – but laminates? I'm leaving it to the professionals.

I cook for him as a thank you, since he only wanted fifty quid for doing the floor. I'm not sure if I offer to cook because he only wants fifty quid and I felt guilty, or because I secretly *want* him to come round for dinner. Either way, I find myself enjoying his company. He is much more attentive than the non-boyfriend, who can't commit to a dinner date booked three weeks in advance, and who I feel constantly let down by.

So, he lays the floor while I cook and we sit in the back bedroom – *still* the only habitable clean space – and eat sausage and mash from little tea tables. After dinner he tries to kiss me but I pull away, still unsure if that's what I want.

He asks me what I *do* want from him.

'I don't know,' I reply, which is the honest answer. All I know is that I still want to see him when he doesn't work for me any more. I know he has a son. I know I must be careful. There is a lot at stake for everyone and I don't want to rush into anything.

I tell him about the non-boyfriend, what he and I have, or rather, what we *don't* have. I tell him that the non-boyfriend never wants children. I tell him that *I* do, or at least I think I do. I am open and honest, laying it on the line so he can walk away from this if he wants to. He winks at me and says he will come round next Sunday to help me put up my furniture. We are friends now, at least.

15th May cont.

As I clunk along in my car, it creaks its discomfort at me. It has never fully recovered from the abuse it received during the renovations, poor thing. I pat the steering wheel as if it has feelings, begging it not to die. I think over those times a lot, those good old early days, and how it was to work alongside the carpenter.

Pausing at a set of traffic lights, my eyes drift down to my kit on the lonely seat beside me, my stomach twisting at the thought of injecting myself again. My eyes blur lazily as I recall the old *us*: mere ghosts against this new strained reality. I wonder if nostalgia will be strong enough to carry us through?

A loud beep from behind brings my unfocused eyes back to the now green traffic lights and I drive on, turning things over in my mind.

We didn't look twice at the new house, we didn't survey it, we just bought it. It was rash, but we were secretly hoping that it would be just like trying to have a baby. We hope that *this* 'baby' might hold us together too. Another plaster.

The IVF dates I've been given today should work out well. Though irritatingly enough, despite trying to engineer it to the contrary, I'm busier than when I was working. It's even been hard trying to fit in my compulsory fortnightly visit to the job centre, though I am grateful that they've finally processed my application. It's taken the heat off me in that regard. It was very difficult trying to explain my situation to them, but they seem satisfied that I have a job to go back to and that I've made some efforts to find temporary work by registering with those marketing people in the interim.

To be honest I could really do without all this extra hassle. If I had known he'd need me to be earning I'd never have come out of work. It was another of those bright ideas that he didn't think through. But anyway, we're in the system now so I'm just trying to roll with it and search for suitable work alongside sorting out the move.

I'm not selling my place to fund the move. I couldn't do it, something stopped me. So, I'm remortgaging and letting it out instead. It means that we can still live in it for a while before a tenant moves in, which makes life a lot easier. You always get so much more done if you're not trying to renovate around yourself. It won't be too long before I'm deep into the IVF and not in any fit state to work on the new place, or really have it going on around me. I must have a clean and clear home by then, for my mind as much as for my body. It is important. He doesn't seem to quite understand this, but I'm hopeful that he will, eventually.

With this treatment cycle I've decided to have acupuncture. I've found a local woman who is a Zita West affiliate, the veritable guru of all things fertility-based. She even has her own vitamin range. That could help, I think. I *hope*.

I stick the radio on. Mellow Magic comes drifting out of the speakers and I try to relax.

It's all been quite stressful, getting the move arranged, sorting through the mountain of jobs that need to be done before it. People don't appreciate why there is such *urgency*, why delays – reasonable or otherwise – send me positively up the wall. The financial advisor's assistant has all but driven me insane. She is condescending and aloof on the phone, which I seriously don't need. I've paid her £400 to administer my case. Administer it! The other day she had the cheek to tell me that she simply didn't have time to put in a very urgent call to the bank to deal with a major problem that had come up – the problem being that she'd applied for the wrong bloody mortgage! I could've *killed* her! She is quite happy to let things drift along at their own sweet pace. Alas the rest of us have houses to buy, destroy and recreate, and babies to bake. I've always made allowances for others when they are going through tough times, why can't she do the same? Can't she comprehend how hard it is to juggle a million things all by myself while also needing to remain ultra calm and *not get stressed*?

I pause my brain for a moment, taking a few deep breaths. It doesn't work. I fail hopelessly at being the embodiment of tranquillity, and revert to imagining myself as a cartoon squirrel, stuck to the giant snowball as it barrels downhill. There's just been *so* much paperwork. The carpenter doesn't do paperwork, so I'm doing everything: the borrowing, the mortgages, the shuffling of finances. The hassle involved in buying a house never fails to amaze me. It should be easy, but it never is.

I really do need to get into that house and get settled. I need to slow down. I need to feel calm, so I can concentrate once more on this big important thing that I'm asking of my heart and body. For now, all I can do is sit and wait it out. So the car and I creak along together, each endeavouring to let Mellow Magic work miracles, as we creep home towards our rather uncertain futures.

10th June

I'm staying at my mum and dad's on a one-night stopover. It'll be a nice change and a welcome relief from all the stress at home, a quick getaway before we are lost to the building works and IVF ICSI. I'm going to a reunion with people I haven't seen in ages, some of them for over ten years. These people knew me before I was married – *either* time. They are from my old life, as I call it. I worked for them for a year here in Leeds before I made the big decision to give the golden streets of London a go. It was my first job out of university.

I am driving up from London via Milton Keynes where I've had to take a minor, yet very irritating, detour to the hospital. I managed to leave the pills I am starting today (the meds start before the needles do) at home. They are the one thing I *had* to remember and the one thing I *cannot* do without. I feel like there's an invisible evil sprite trying to thwart me. The pills are just a version of the contraceptive pill, but it's as if I'm asking for methadone. Thankfully, after much debate, the hospital decides they'll be able to search my now nationally computerised medical notes for a record of them. They find the prescription, though it does seem to take forever, and go off to the pharmacy to get them for me.

It's rather ironic that the pre-treatment medication for IVF is something designed specifically to *stop* you getting pregnant. They say it stops you developing any ovarian cysts. These are something you must be clear of before you can start injecting the downregulation drugs which make your lady-innards inactive (making you feel menopausal and suicidal in the process) before finally moving onto the stimulation drugs that send your ovaries into overdrive. So you have to de-cyst, de-activate then over-activate. How wonderfully confusing for your body. God, I'm so bored of talking about cysts and ovaries, uterus linings and sperm quality. Why is it all so clinical? I'm busy pulling faces at the thought of all this when the doctor comes out, finally furnishing me with the necessary drugs.

I jump back in the car and stick on my 'Belief, Bump, Baby!' CD for a bit of positive light relief, before remembering that this is a hypnosis CD and I am, in fact, *driving the car.* I switch it off hastily, staring instead at the monotonous grey of the road ahead. But, very soon, my mind wanders back to the treatment and how tedious it all is: how complex, awkward and unnatural. Having a baby is the very thing that's supposed to make you feel like a woman, but this is making me feel androgenised, it's so undignified and unsavoury. I'm sick to death of thinking about it. I want to think about baby clothes, maternity wear, scans and neo-natal appointments, but instead I get needles, cysts and ovary function.

Standing on the edge of it all again, somewhere in the middle of reunion parties, renovations, IVF nurses, in between hopefulness and sadness, I find it hard to see where I fit in with life. There are two possible lives ahead of me and I just don't know which one I'm going to get. Today is day one of the treatment. The walk to the end of the road looks very, *very* long – and I'm not entirely sure I'm wearing the best shoes for it.

I arrive at the reunion and walk into the building, breathing in the overwhelming smell of office carpet and damp northern stone. And it's like I was here only yesterday. I feel invigorated and suddenly quite cross with myself that I didn't stick it out, hold on and stay up here. Perhaps I would have been happier? Perhaps...

I search for my friends and see a few familiar smiles, but the faces are mostly new. There are ten years of people I don't know and somehow I don't quite fit in, though I really want to. I put my best foot forward, smile and cross the room. I catch the eye of two old friends and we squish in next to each other at the makeshift bar. It's good to catch up, to talk, especially to people who don't greet me with the sympathetic head tilt that no one seems able to avoid these days. It is refreshing to be *just me* for a change, not someone's wife or patient. I want to belong somewhere. I want to remember my dreams again – the other ones that didn't involve babies. But conversation dries up after a time and I realise that I barely lived this life. I moved on from it so quickly that it feels a little clunky, it's not flowing naturally. It isn't because I'm not wanted here, wasn't popular or good enough at my job, it's just that a lot of time has passed. It's as if I am trying on an old, forgotten, pair of slippers, which I've found at the bottom of my wardrobe. I feel as if I *could* belong here, where my blunt northern-ness, in both character and voice, is welcomed and embraced, not squashed, ridiculed or seen as something to be hidden. It is another of the lives I might have had, *still could* have, if I decided to change it all again...

The part of me that wants to fit in somewhere flutters against my chest, frantically trying to beat its way out, desperate for something to clutch on to.

Later on, I find myself crying as I drive over to Mum and Dad's. I am so bored of crying. The weather is dreadful and I can't see the road markings for the tears, and the slosh and fizz of the rain. I'm crying because I feel left behind again. Almost all my friends have children now and I can't keep up with them. I can't fully relate to their mummy world. Some have disconnected altogether – I am not in their special club. This is not true of my *best* friends, my dear friends, but even with them I feel I will never be on an equal footing with no child of my own.

I arrive at my parents' house and turn off the engine. I stare out of the window for a while as the rain pours down, enjoying the funny sort of non-silent silence it brings. Then I let myself in quietly and go up to bed, not entirely sure how I'm feeling any more, other than being completely drained and ready to land on my old bed in a heap. I trudge up the stairs and there, on my old bed from my old life, is my little old dog, waiting for me. Feeling instantly better, I flop down beside her and she licks my face clean. And I know that at least I will always fit in here.

14th June

I pull into the driveway of a large, privately owned house. It seems much like any other around here, except this house holds the key to my fate – or so my fertility guidebook would have me believe. I have read it cover to cover, twice.

The house has a grand sort of entrance with two front doors leading on to the same hall. I think at some point it must have been converted into flats and then later put back to its original state, leaving just the two-door entrance as a scar on the building. I ring the bell and am invited inside by a lady with a limp, wearing a nurse's uniform. She has one of those slightly ethereal voices that people who work in day spas use and she coos at me to take a seat. The acupuncturist will be along shortly.

I am nervous. The house smells of English Heritage properties and old tapestries and the air has a feel about it as if it too is as ancient as the art of acupuncture. I can hear nothing but the faint 'vrum' of cars driving past outside. It doesn't exactly feel *relaxing* here, although I think it's meant to, but it does feel *still* and peaceful, as if someone has paused time.

The lady with the ethereal voice pops in and out of the various little rooms off the main hallway, tending to whoever is currently pinned in inside them. She shows me to a funny little room with French doors that lead on to a pleasant garden, leaving me to take off my jeans and lie down on the bed.

I stare at the ceiling, trying to suppress any negativity I may have dragged into the room with me, listening to the birds trilling outside.

The acupuncturist finally comes in and asks me why I am here and what she can do to help. Such a simple question.

'I'm trying to have a baby,' I tell her, and a little lump catches in my throat. 'We're having IVF, well IVF ICSI.'

She folds her hands and tilts her head sympathetically.

'It's not me, it's him, but we've had one round already and it didn't work and I just want to try everything I can.'

More little lumps catch in my throat. She smiles and tilts her head further, and before I can stop them, the tears are out of my eyes and down my face. I instantly feel exhausted. My mouth turns down at the corners, my lips quiver, and I am undone.

The acupuncturist doesn't change her expression, but she does come over and put her arm round me. It is quite soothing. My heart is so sore still and I realise it hasn't taken much to push me over the edge again. I want this ache to go away. I want so much to feel some relief from its nag, but here it is, ever present, and I say it out loud.

'He doesn't really want a baby.'

She asks our ages. I tell her. Then she purses her lips a little and asks if he's always not wanted a baby. Didn't we both think that he'd love the baby once it was here? She wants me to explain how we've come to be having IVF ICSI.

I tell her the short version from the beginning. I make it sound so simple, despite it feeling like we're tied in a million tricky little knots. I tell her that the carpenter keeps changing his mind, back and forth. I say that I feel under such pressure to do this thing *now*, quickly, before I lose

126

him on it altogether and seal my fate as being childless forever.

She says this is a lot for me to bear. She says he is not being kind or supportive but perhaps he doesn't know how to be.

I mull this over and decide quickly that it must be the case. How can someone claim to love you and behave in the way that he has?

The acupuncturist asks me, as I lie back down, what it was that attracted me to him in the first place, but I can't think of an answer. My mind is blank. I simply can't remember. I don't know any more.

She feels sorry for me, but neither she nor I can change him and other than offering a comforting arm, some well thought out words, and a load of pins, she can't really help me. I'm on my own.

The acupuncturist explains what she is about to do. She says there will be a few variations on a theme with the acupuncture, depending on what we are trying to achieve relative to where I'm at in my cycle, and at what stage of the treatment I'm in. She wants to get my body attuned, to stimulate it to do all the right things at the right times and encourage it to be the best it can be. She says to relax and that it won't hurt. This turns out to be a total lie. It hurts like hell. Each little pinprick sends hot electricity up and down my body, shooting pain everywhere and I feel unbelievably emotional. The points where the pins go in throb horribly and the more pins she puts in, the more tense I can feel myself getting. How can anyone possibly find this relaxing? I'm not disputing the other potential benefits, but relaxing it is not!

She leaves me alone to settle down and I realise I've left my hypnosis CD in my bag. I try to get up and fetch it. This is a *big* mistake. The pain points scream out at me loudly and I lay there stunned and a bit horrified. What if there was a fire? I'd be effectively pinioned to the bed! I try to listen to the birdsong outside instead, which is still pouring in through the glass doors, along with a shaft of brilliant sunlight. I close my eyes and try to drift off to that place under the water, hoping my body is understanding of the pins and their point.

I come round about twenty minutes later, having dozed off and, surprisingly, I actually *do* feel quite relaxed now. The acupuncturist quickly removes the needles, causing only a fraction of the pain, and I get a nice massage – which is by far the most enjoyable part of the whole affair.

I get dressed and wander into the hallway again, where I am told that the acupuncturist will see me twice a week, then once on the day of egg collection and twice on the day of the embryo transfer, once before it and once after.

I gulp quietly as I think of the huge cost involved, but shake this off as I hand over my credit card, mentally repeating my mantra: I must give us the best possible chance. I will worry about the money later.

I daren't ask for money from the carpenter for the acupuncture. I'm not entirely sure how he thinks I'm paying for it, but he doesn't ask. Anyway, the money is unimportant, ultimately. I must do everything within my power to help us have a good shot at the IVF this time.

The carpenter, despite everything, is at least making a show of trying to do his bit. He is taking special supplements and drinking less alcohol too, which I must say is a *joy*. He is a totally different person when he doesn't drink and I'm enjoying life without his alter ego. Plus, the closer we get to completing on the house, the brighter he seems to get about everything. This is because he is getting something he very much wants: a big house to destroy and rebuild. His *dream* home no less: four beds, two baths, a nice garden and a garage... Suburban bliss. Our new chapter is beginning, we are moving forward in our lives, and I do feel that we are steadier at the moment. Perhaps it is just the prospect of the house that has altered him? Or maybe he *is* actually coming back round to the baby idea? Whichever it is, the carpenter and I have dragged ourselves back together. What was rocky over the last *many* months feels more even, as if this horrid thing that has happened had a purpose, that it was meant to save us somehow, and that we want the same things again.

We are so excited to be renovating soon. And perhaps the physical labour of it all – the sweat and love we will pour into it, the floors we will sand (together!), the new cabinets he will build – will be like us starting again. Perhaps everything else will be better for our fresh start too – maybe he'll be happier with the treatment this time around. Maybe he'll be there for me. Maybe the acupuncturist was right, he just didn't know *how* to before.

30th June

We finally have the keys to our new house. It feels like I've been waiting impatiently for this day for so much longer than I actually have. I've been desperately craving the clarity of this set event as a contrast to the uncertainty of the IVF – and our future. I've been dying to get into the place and rip down some walls, to get on with the decorating. I've been fervently collecting colour swatches from the Dulux counter, fawning over them as if they hold special powers. And I'm sick to the back teeth of sorting out finances, jumping through a multitude of hoops, fulfilling criteria to prove that we can afford what we're already paying out.

I'm feeling very positive. My mood is reflected by the sunny weather, and I arrive at the property cheerful – despite the drab grey pebbledashing. But when I get to our new front door, I can't work the lock, which is clearly *not* a great start. Hoping that this it is not a bad sign, I jiggle the key in the lock for a full twenty minutes, holding the phone under my chin. The estate agent is on the other end of the line, trying to deliver instructions on how to gain entry and I'm just about to give up and ask them to come and do it for me when, mercifully, the door pings open.

I hang up and wander in, the dreadful décor slapping me in the face again. I throw my bag on the floor and have a good nose around. The house smells of other people: their perfumes, washing powders and cooking – innocuous enough but distinct. The previous owner has left an assortment of useful manuals and guarantees in a handy little folder, all neatly labelled. Unfortunately he's also been kind enough to leave a large shoebox full of porn hidden in the loft. I put it to one side and get stuck in to the DIY, ripping out the old kitchen units (MFI circa 1988 'monstrosity' variety) and cart them off to the tip. It takes several trips, and it is with some satisfaction and relish that I javelin, shot-put and generally hurl the offending lumps of wood far into the skips at the other end. We have begun.

The carpenter should be home at any minute. He's only doing a half-day today. My efforts with the kitchen have pushed me to that sweaty, giddy place where I want nothing more than to tirelessly plan and paint.

He arrives, and we bounce around inside our new bricks as if we're on fast forward, strategising excitedly. We are talking *at* each other, over each other. He is formulating plans to move walls and change layouts; I am mentally choosing wallpaper and shopping for curtains...

I pause for thought and breath, he does not, and I watch

him as he dervishes his way around the rooms, cheerfully measuring and drawing. I have never seen him quite so animated. Actually that isn't true, I haven't seen him this animated since the last time. He was never so vibrant as when we first met and worked on my place together, and until very recently he has been a shell of a person. Our life together hasn't been enough to raise so much as a cheeky grin out of him of late and I can't help thinking that perhaps *I* am simply not enough to get excited about any more. Perhaps I need to come with a building project attached? Still, watching him makes me smile. The smile spreads through me as the sun pours through the windows, warm and genuine. It is a relief. I remember when we were happy. I remember the day I *knew*...

Then

It is midday on the long-awaited non-boyfriend Sunday. The carpenter has come round to help with the big furniture as promised. He is chipper. I am not.

The non-boyfriend has cancelled on me. I am cross and hurt and I feel, as I so often do, completely let down by him. And I know that, really, it is over between us. I can't go on with the uncertainty of it any more – the ups and downs (mostly the downs), the not knowing when I'm going to see him next. He meant a lot to me but this isn't what I want. I want a relationship. And he can't even keep a date with me.

So I decide something on the spur of the moment. I decide I like someone else.

I ask the carpenter if he wants to help me sort out a few things in town, saying that I could use the company. He could help me carry stuff if he likes. I am inviting him into my life. Somehow I'd rather spend the day with this man than even *be* with the non-boyfriend. I see that the carpenter could commit. *He* wants a relationship and it is now that I let one develop.

We eat porridge standing up in the kitchen. I make it the special way my grandma taught me, with nutmeg and raisins, and we chat over two full pots of tea before hopping in the car. He comes with me to Next to pick out shelves, and we meander round the homeware department casually, as if this is something we do every weekend. It doesn't feel awkward or clunky in any way; there are no tumbleweed-inducing silences. It feels nothing more or less than *normal*, which is somehow quite exciting. I buy what I need, we go to Homebase, then on to the curtain shop.

I walk in and spot them immediately: the right curtains. I am about to ask the carpenter's opinion – are they too neutral for a living room? – but before the words are out of my mouth, he points at them and says, 'Those would go really well with your sofa, babes.'

Destiny takes over. We walk into the shop, I pick up the curtains, pay for them and, somehow, we leave as a couple. We are together. There's always a tipping point. For us, the curtains did it.

We spend the night together. And it feels safe. Natural. Like it has always been. I drift off to sleep under his arm, but wake up alone in the early hours – he had to go back to his son – and I am sad he is not here.

Now

We've been working long and late and I've barely had time to think. Certainly I've been sleeping better. There have been no disturbing dreams of bumps and babies, just sheer, unadulterated, exhausted sleep. I haven't thought, I have just *done*: worked, drunk tea, slept. I must have eaten but I forget when. I am feeling a bit more with it. I have built up some stamina and am not behaving like a robot any more. A little bit of my personality has returned.

We've ripped down the wall between the bathroom and the loo to create one mega room. The carpenter shares my vision of a hotel-style bathroom with mosaic tiles, a double bath and a showerhead the size of a dinner plate. Then, there are more walls to come down, a kitchen to build from scratch and another chimney to excavate. I've bought a beautiful art deco fireplace from a reclamation yard that I can't wait to see *in situ*. I've spent hours lovingly restoring it and I am beside myself with delight at the result of my efforts.

There are workmen all around us. A representative of every trade under the sun has been drafted in and I really do feel like I'm on one of those DIY reality TV shows. I've never made so much tea – nor has the stepson. He's here in the chaos with us, doing his very best to help. I don't think he's ever slogged it out quite so much but, true to form, he remains very upbeat about the hard work and long hours. And he is keeping a close eye on me, making sure I'm all right and that I'm eating properly. I really do love him. If the carpenter and I have a boy, I want him to be just like the stepson. We have such a good bond and – even though he isn't – it feels just a little bit like he's my own.

The carpenter sees how close we are and he's genuinely happy that we have such a strong relationship. It goes some way towards holding our own together.

This afternoon, I find myself sitting at the top of a ladder painting away and the carpenter climbs up to meet me, kissing my face. I love it when he is happy and smiling his silly, crooked smile. I feel like he comes back to me in moments like these. It is how we always used to be: filthy, up to our necks in it, but smiling. We need to get back to who we were when we started.

For the best part I am very content, but time is at our heels. I'm starting to long for a full day off and a little bit of rest, but we must keep going if we're to get everything done in time. My only time of proper relaxation, if you can call it that, is at the acupuncturist.

The acupuncture *is* helping, though, I think. I feel calmer in myself, or least I do at times. I am conscious of doing too much at the house, but I also feel that if I don't dig deep and keep pushing, the carpenter might sit back too and we can't afford to waste time. We are in this together, ploughing through the messy stuff.

I do like this world, with dirt and rubble and builders everywhere. I am comfortable around these people who graft all week in extremely good humour and horrid conditions. I will remember them the next time I hear someone bitching that they are still in the office photocopying things at 5.00pm – not that I'll be seeing any offices or photocopiers any time soon. My sabbatical is still in place and they are not expecting me back until the first week in September. They say they can't extend the sabbatical if our treatment is delayed or fails again. More worryingly, it seems they are getting along just fine without me, using the unpaid intern... But I've made my choice and I feel like I'm doing the right thing: devoting my time and efforts to our family, our big build, and *us*.

I'm almost at the end of the pills now. I start injecting again very soon, so we must get the job finished by then, at least to a point where the house is 'liveable-inable'. The carpenter still doesn't quite understand why it can't be a building site when those big drugs start and he's ever so slightly grumpy because of my doggedness. But those drugs drain you, they do. I won't be fit to do anything much once I'm injecting those into my system. He remains blinkered about the full strain and impact this treatment has on me and indeed, through choice or ignorance, completely fails to see how much support and buoying up I need from him on that front. That is *his* role in it, and it is a vital one.

I hope that maybe, as we go through all this again, we can leave behind our old war wounds and finally heal. Or will the giant baby-shaped cracks in our relationship still be there, hovering nearby, just aching to find their way back in, never quite far enough in the past to be gone?

11th July

The builders have gone and the furniture is in. Moving day came and went without incident. Thankfully the carpenter, after much persuading, agreed to let me get a removals company in, so most of the hard stuff was done for us. I just couldn't face doing it over dozens of trips in his little van, it would've taken forever! It was so nice to sit back and let 'the boys' get on with it, a real treat before life stops once more.

The injecting has begun. It doesn't overwhelm me quite as much as last time, though it still brings me out in cold sweats. I expect it to hurt and know it's just another unpleasant reality of our situation, but I do hate this part – not that any part is pleasant – and just looking at the bare needle makes me feel nauseous. I sit up each morning in bed at 7.00am and hold an ice pack to my stomach, hypodermic prepped and ready. Once my skin is cold, I sit for what seems like an age, plucking up the courage to push the needle in. It's harder than you'd think, your skin. There's a surprising amount of resistance. You'd think the needle would slip right in, like a clichéd hot knife through butter, but it's actually a bit closer to pushing a corn skewer into an orange. And then there's that nasty sting as you push the plunger down... It's not like you can even look away. It makes me feel faint. But I push myself through it for the cause.

As the days go by, I can feel myself sinking beneath the sad grey cloud that the drugs induce and I have to fight to stay positive. I see so many people around me achieving pregnancy with ease. Even those doing it artificially seem to be successful by the barrowload. It's funny. Well, I say funny. It's actually not very funny at all. Not for me, not really. It's sort of depressing. Here I am, married, with a fabulous new house (which is *almost* 'liveable-inable') and the final piece of the jigsaw puzzle eludes us. I know there will be a million other women out there, going through the same thing. I know I'm not the only one, and that I should just count my blessings and be grateful, but it all seems *desperately* unfair.

I tried looking into the nitty-gritty of getting pregnant, to see if there was anything I might be missing, any little tricks that I could try. But all I discovered was that getting pregnant is actually rather hard and highly improbable. I've watched enough documentaries to know. You've got to have exactly the right timing between ovulation and sex, just the right uterine conditions, the right sperm, the right egg, the right implantation location. They claim that only about twenty swimmers make it past your sperm-killing vagina. Seriously, your vagina *actually* kills them off. What a terrific design! The poor few tired little guys that make the swim then have to try to burrow into the egg – if there's even one there! That's like asking someone to go potholing at the end of a triathlon in a cave that's only there for a few days every month. None of this knowledge has made me feel any better whatsoever and it's just made my situation seem all the more stark. It's not as if we're off to a winning start or have any kind of advantage. How are so many people getting their babies when the odds against it are so stacked? It's a bloody miracle. How do the teenage mothers you hear about get pregnant on go one?

I asked my specialist this question when I saw him yesterday. He said that very young women could ovulate as much as twice a month and that they also have a larger *window*. I was a little baffled by this, wondering if I'd somehow slipped into discussing our new UPVC box sashes inadvertently – the house still consumes so much of my mind.

'They have a large fertile window when the cervical mucus is flowing,' he explained. 'This is the only mucus that the sperm can swim up through. Younger women have more of it, more regularly. So it's far easier for them to get pregnant.'

I pulled a distinctly repulsed expression as my brain added *mucus* to my list of words appropriate to clinical babydom. Honestly, you go your whole life believing you'll create a little person in a moment of sparkling desire, only to learn that, no, you're one of the lucky ones who get to do it via a uterine catheter and have your baby 'administered' by a man in a white coat with your privates splayed open for the whole room to see. All I could think of on the way home was: Brilliant. I have no mucus and a small window. Maybe I can simply get a new one fitted? I'm sure I still have the brochure somewhere.

14th July

The days pass dully and slowly and I sit, blank-faced, under my little cloud. The carpenter is suddenly less than understanding and chooses to ignore my moodiness – and me. It's not what I want from him, but it's probably for the best, in truth.

The hospital scans me to see if everything is reacting normally, which it is. This is some consolation for how miserable I feel. The scans are so invasive. They try to make it as pleasant an experience as possible, although it's hard to disguise the fact that they're about to shove a great probe up your vagina and prod you in the ovaries. There's only so 'nice' they can make it. But it's a necessary evil and actually quite interesting to see your insides displayed on a computer screen. Perhaps next time I should take popcorn?

I know I would feel totally different about the whole affair (depressing drugs aside) if the image looking back at me was of a little beating heart. I would give almost anything to see that now. It is the thought of it that pushes me on, making me get up, ice and inject – even though it the equivalent of forcing yourself to eat something that you know will make you ill.

21st July

After an eternity of sluggish, protracted days, I've finished the downregulation drugs and I'm on to the stimulation phase. Even though I'm having to give myself two injections a day now, I feel better for the change in medication already, just like before: instantly lifted from under my little grey cloud.

I've felt utterly belligerent and depressed up to this point and I'm relieved to be feeling more like myself. I could barely face so much as lifting the TV remote these last days. But things have been going well, medically speaking, and the scans I've had to drag myself out of the house for have shown the right progress, so at least I don't have to *stay* on the nasty drugs. My body is responding well.

To further assist my lift of mood, I have finally, thankfully, landed some work. I might be mid-IVF and mid-renovations, but we also need to eat, so I am relieved. Taking a sabbatical from work has been as much a huge mistake as it has been useful. Claiming benefits has been something of an eye opener and a fairly ugly experience. It seriously hasn't helped my moods. I know I'm no freeloader, yet I feel like a burden on society. I *shouldn't* feel ashamed, but I do every time I go down there. It's a horrid feeling and it creeps over me as I climb the little hill to the job centre every other Tuesday.

Then

Two telephones ring at the same time. My favourite work friend grabs them both, one in each hand, then has a moment of bewildered panic as she decides who to speak to first. It's like the stock exchange in here! I'm holding a phone in one hand and waving madly with the other one at the head agent – who is *still* dealing with a contract renegotiation with the BBC, with no sign of a deal yet. I restart the hold music for the man from the *Daily Mail* who is currently in phone purgatory on line 1.

It's 30 degrees: oppressive and exhausting. I'm quite sure at any moment I shall melt into the new carpet. The office is positively airless despite our attempts to throw the window wide open. The air-con man is downstairs trying to free us from our slow deaths. How I long for glacial... Anything but this!

I can't get a single thing done, including the wages – and they're a priority. The room in veritably buzzing. We're all supposed to be going out tonight to mark the opening of a new show. We're totally up against it – but we can't cancel, so anything vital that doesn't get done today will have to carry over. Everyone is on overdrive. The girl in admin is almost in tears over the Stage Awards ceremony she's attempting to throw together.

I look around the room and realise I'll have to ring the carpenter and move tomorrow's date. Perhaps we can do something at the weekend instead. Weekdays are just to full right now to try to have any other kind of actual life.

The head agent suddenly frees up and I quickly patch through the *Daily Mail* man. The intercom goes. I let in a sweltering courier and hurriedly sign for the package, then pop over and plop whatever it is on the agent's desk, as he gruffly hangs up the phone. It's been a tough morning. The press are hounding us, chasing the low-down on the antics of a particularly wayward client and we can't seem to shake them off.

The head agent raises his eyebrows in a 'What the hell do we do?' kind of way as he rips open the package. He takes one startled look at the contents and grabs the phone again. Quite sure I just saw half a picture of a naked boob, I smile and run for cover... I love my job.

I sit in the job centre, being judged by the staff, whose main aim seems to be to weed out benefit cheats rather than offer real job-seeking support. As they scrutinise my weekly logged efforts to find employment it's as if they are permanently on guard – trying to trip me up, catch me out and cut me off, and I am constantly terrified of saying the wrong thing. I had thought there would be some compassion, but no. I am part of the system now and they want to get me into work – *any* work – and off their hands as quickly as possible. It doesn't matter whether the job is a good one, whether I am suitable for it or the other way around, they just want to get rid of me. They are quite condescending and it does irritate me. I have worked solidly for over a decade, putting in my monthly contribution, and now here I sit, being patronised and made to feel guilty for my current situation.

We 'clients', as the job centre calls us, are a real mixed bunch, each with our own strange subcategory of situation to explain, and be assisted through, as our confidence dribbles away. I watch the others avidly each week: the kids who just can't get that first job, the people who are too old to be appealing to an employer, the ones who've been made redundant, the housewives returning to work – and me. We are all dutifully trying so hard to fill this hole in our lives. There are some who are trapped in the system, falling foul of its flaws. They get stuck because the system cuts you off so immediately when you *do* get work that there is no buffer, no money for the time between benefit cheque and payday, to live on. These are the people I feel sorry for the most. They want to work, but the system seems to work against them. It makes them better off if they stay on benefit. And then there are the others, the handful of repeat customers who seem able to play the system beautifully, leaping effortlessly through the various loopholes, happily living forever more on the money they get. The rest of us watch them in horror – we can't quite bear it, but we somehow can't quite peel our eyes away either. It must be what it's like to work on the Jeremy Kyle show.

But today, I'm *not* at the job centre. Today, I am busy outside doing my job. And I'm making great efforts to appear very focused. But to be honest, I'm quite distracted. I can do nothing but *stare*. It seems as if the entire world is to be kept populated solely by the people of Donwich. The area around the new grocery store at the top of Lords Lane is a particular treat because at least every other woman is 'with child'.

I'm only here for a brief four days, but this is not, it seems, brief enough for the job centre not to cut me off at source. I've been unceremoniously catapulted off jobseeker's allowance for these four days and told I will have to claim again on Monday (God help me). This claim could take up to two weeks to be evaluated. What I'm supposed to do in the interim I'm not entirely sure. I don't get paid for these four days' work for another month, so it feels as thought I am losing out all round.

It's not *particularly* great timing for me to be doing this sort of work either, as it means being on my feet all day and I'm getting sore as my ever-increasing ovaries swell. Still, I'm remaining positive. I've continued to enjoy my bi-weekly sessions with the acupuncturist, which haven't got any less tense, though I always feel more chilled afterwards. It's a very strange thing, acupuncture. I have another scan coming up in a few days to see how many follicles there are on my ovaries, how many potential eggs. They want to make sure I'm not *over*-stimulated and won't, therefore, drop dead...

My ovaries and me have been busily handing out balloons and leaflets in a far too fake and chirpy manner, which has all but vanished by 2.00pm. I'm knackered and my demeanour is peppered with tiredness and a certain amount of humiliation. Not because I'm above such things. On the contrary, the money is good and it really is quite a jolly little job, despite my moaning. No, I'm embarrassed because I've had to do the ballooning in a neon green T-shirt with a matching baseball cap and sash, complete with the shop logo emblazoned across it. And as I pound the pavements, there they all are, the yummy mummies to be, eating eggs benedict and buying food from the lovely local delis. They are *not* wearing neon green T-shirts but waddling daintily around, popping into the Oliver Bonas sale for a quick look. The entire neighbourhood is thronged with babies, bumps and buggies and here I am, in the middle of it all, no bump in sight, fighting with my swollen ovaries – and giving out balloons to everyone else's children. Posh, spoilt, delightful and charming, they are all out and they are all *immaculate* with their White Stuff clothes and perfectly braided hair. Should I feel like I am in some sort of hell? It makes me wonder if Donwich is secretly quite a boring place to live, so nobody has anything to do over the winter months except have sex.

But as the day goes on, the babymania of Donwich starts to make me feel like I am in the special club too. At first, I felt more and more excluded with every additional bump I saw, but now I've decided that I can either make it hell for myself (and everyone else) or get on board and feel like I'm the next pregnant belly in line. I can almost see it: me in six months' time, walking hand in hand with the carpenter through Donwich, enjoying the sunshine and delis with all the other bumps...

I dash into White Stuff and spend a hundred quid I haven't got on my credit card and I am as high as a kite. I feel like I fit in. The bumps have made me shop! I even buy a couple of tops with growing room.

At the end of the day, I give back my giant green T-shirt and stick on one of the tops I've just bought. Then I walk towards my car as one of *them*. I'm nearly there! I just need to swap my giant ovaries for a beautiful bump, and maybe move to Donwich...

27th July

And so it begins. I'm uncomfortable. All of a sudden I've gone from being fine to being *really* uncomfortable. I'm well into the stimulation phase, and my belly is distended and sore. I'm literally swelling up. I ring the acupuncturist to see if there's anything she can do to calm things down as things are taking their toll. I make an appointment.

Today, I've had one more day of employment, handing out ice cream samples at the annual New Forest Show. I secretly hope this is going to be it for a while. It took me an age to get there and I was as uncomfortable sitting in the car, roasting, as I was standing on my feet all day when I got there. But at least the T-shirts weren't green this time and I quite enjoyed the change of scene. It brought with it some welcome respite.

The carpenter and I had had an argument about babies this morning. He has started to put it out there again that he really doesn't want to do the IVF. I'm not sure I want to have a baby with someone who doesn't want one – who would? It doesn't bear thinking about, and yet I have to. He continually says that I must not expect him to be excited about it, and so *my* excitement is crushed by his heavy unwanted words. Some days he seems to be with me – just the other day he wanted to go look at buggies – then he does *this*. Again. He is so contradictory. I don't know why he is saying this *now*, when we're actually in the middle of it all (somewhat committed!) and I'm drugged up to the eyeballs...

The sunshine and the New Forest air did me good though, and at least it got me out of the house. The man who ran our stand was lovely. He's an older dad at 50, with young twins by IVF ICSI, funnily enough, so we had plenty to talk about and it was quite good to hear his side of things. His wife is only a touch older than I am at 34, and their age gap is much bigger than the carpenter's and mine. I told him about the fight, about everything at home. I told him how one day the carpenter says he wants to try again, and then the next day says he doesn't want kids at all any more, but that he'll do it for me, even though he begrudges it. How he says that it has to be *my* baby.

The man said that he was apprehensive too and that it is a daunting prospect, having to start that part of your life all over again. I pointed out that the carpenter never needed to make those promises to me, he *chose* to. The man agreed it must be tough for me, but he could see both sides. Perhaps I can understand the carpenter's side a little better, too, for having talked to him. He gave me a glimmer of hope when he told me his wife had *insisted* they try (it was her deal-breaker) but he now feels like a spring chicken. It's the best thing he's ever done. I hope the carpenter will feel like this when we get *our* baby.

28th July

My discomfort is significantly worse than the last time.

I went for a scan this morning. I got up, drove for about ten minutes, lay on my back for a further ten while the nurse poked around, then drove home. And I am completely wiped out. I just feel so tired all the time. I have to drink enormous amounts of water to reduce retention, as the drugs put you at risk of laying fluid down on your lungs – yet another potential treat I could get from all this. I've taken to drinking lots of coconut water too (a trick I learned about online), which is really helping, though it makes me have to pee constantly – which means I have to keep dragging myself off the sofa and up the stairs. The online forums are something I am constantly cruising again, finding support in their pages from people I don't know. Support is something I wish I had outside of cyberspace, but asking for it at home risks sending my husband into meltdown, so I don't bother.

It is *ridiculously* hot. I'm wearing nothing but a bra-top and knickers, but I'm still sweaty and stuck to the settee. This morning was the second of my three scans. I have a staggering 33 follicles, split between my two ovaries. There may or may not be an egg in each one, but with that many it's no wonder I'm as sore as hell and my ovaries no longer seem to fit in my body. It's like they're just floating around, too large to sit in their proper place.

Thirty three follicles is a bit *too* high. It could put me at risk of ovarian hyper-stimulation syndrome, a dangerous condition and something I was on the edge of last time. So they've done blood tests and, as the hormone readings are quite elevated, reduced my drug dosages. I'm scared. I tell the carpenter what's happening when he comes home. He looks at me blankly. I stare back and await a response. He says to rest up and goes off to the kitchen to make a tea. I feel that twist of disappointment at his lack of interest and understanding of the situation, but I shake it off. I'm still going for my appointments alone, but he has promised to come to the embryo transfer with me. I don't want to make a fuss. I just try to lie as still as possible and do as he's said: rest.

I manage to drop off for a short while and I drift into my happy underwater world where it is warm and safe. We are both there, the carpenter and I. We have with us a beautiful smiling baby who clings onto my fingers as he swims effortlessly alongside us, our very own water baby. The sunlight pierces the water in a thousand shafts of brilliant, shining, white light. I look around at all the pretty fish that have joined us as they dart through the rays, but when I turn back, the carpenter's face has changed and twisted into the face of gnarled old tree. He smiles a crooked smile and makes a grab for the baby. I reach out through the water to save my precious child... and the phone wakes me up.

It is the hospital, the specialist calling me after seeing my latest results. He sounds worried. If things don't settle down then the cycle might have to be abandoned entirely. I am at *high* risk of hyperstimulation – not the worst-case scenario but it needs bringing under control. He says that if they were to take the eggs out with me at this level it could tip me over the edge. It could even kill me.

It could all have been for nothing. But I *feel* fine, all things considered. I don't feel ill, just massively uncomfortable and bloated. They go on to explain that the hormone you inject to mature your eggs, 36 hours before their removal, sets in motion a chain of reactions that can't be stopped once they get going. Once the eggs are matured then they *must* come out and it is *this* that can put you in danger. It pushes your hormone levels up even further. We have to decide before that injection needs to be given if we are going to continue or not.

The word 'decide' is a horrible one to me at this point in my life. *Decide*. It should suggest a choice, but to me it suggests a finality. I don't know how many more decisions I can make. I don't know what to pick any more, what is for the best: *my* best, *our* best, *his* best?

Choose. Choose between what, one thing and another?

How many rounds? One? Two? Three? Give up? Keep going? One embryo or two? Between one embryo and another?

Which future? Have a child? Have a husband? Have both? Have neither? Be half supported, half happy, half lonely?

It reminds me of another decision about what to keep and what not to – on the first cycle when I had to make that awful phone call. It doesn't take much for it to come flooding back. The colours, the smells... everything...

Then

I ring the carpenter from the waiting room at the hospital. I am extremely tense – things are awful between us at the moment. I have no signal on my own phone so I'm making the call from reception. And everyone can hear me. I am nervous and the public setting makes me upset.

The two embryos that are left out of the few eggs that fertilised – the only two that have actually made it through – could both go back inside me, but neither are good enough to freeze. If we want to save both they must both go back in. This will give us a 40% chance of one baby. They are smiling when they say this, as if the odds are good. I think they're trying to make me feel better.

If I choose to have one put back it means that, not only do we have only a 20% chance and nothing to fall back on should the cycle fail, but that I have to select one. I call the carpenter, as I don't know what I should do. I feel I must ask him, this is something we should discuss. I tell him what they've said, adding: 'They're advising us to put both embryos back.' My heart is racing and I feel positively sick as I wait for his reply.

The line is silent for a long time, so long that I'm not sure he's still there. When he does speak it is with a dangerous tone that he reserves for when he is especially irritated.

'I won't risk having twins,' he says. 'I've already told you, babes. If it were up to me, I'd have no babies at all. I don't really want *any* babies.'

His volume level is far from subtle and I'm sure other people can hear him. I'm becoming embarrassed and tearful.

'I don't know why you're even calling,' he adds.

I tell him it is because this is not an easy, clear-cut decision, that we should be open to all our options and discuss them. These are not decisions I can make alone, nor should I have to.

He says he doesn't want to get involved with it and that he has nothing more to say.

I hang up and go back into theatre. They are waiting on me and they don't have all day.

I push through the door and the team ask me what we have decided. I tell them, managing to keep my mounting sadness from spilling over. I have to pick one to keep and one to flush away. How does a person decide that? They are both just as good as each other, they say, so it doesn't matter. I can just choose, or they can choose for me if I'd prefer. Somehow this seems worse and so I take the gamble with my life and these two little ones and I pick the one on the left.

And I am alone in it.

Now

Back in the present, stuck to the sofa on this very hot day, on hold with the hospital, I realise that I am still a little haunted by that day. This time it is my own health, *my* life at stake. If we choose poorly it could have very serious ramifications for *me*. I feel panicked. But I can't abandon it. I just can't. I can't think that there will be any more attempts at this. The cycle will be abandoned and nearly £800 worth of drugs will have been, effectively, chucked down the drain – just like that other little life.

And if he does agree to give it one more go, if I find a way? We'll have to wait for months before we can start again, and I don't truthfully know if we have months left. I want to believe we can hold our marriage together, but I'm not sure if we'll survive another hairpin bend, as he slowly changes back into that hideous, disconnected person.

The doctor comes back on the phone, just as the hold music has successfully set my teeth on edge. We talk about what options I *do* have. About the possibility of retrieving the eggs, fertilising them and then freezing them all, then putting them back at later dates on a normal period cycle, to allow me to recover. I say that this might be okay – but then I add that if I feel well enough, if I am a borderline case and not in *huge* danger, then I want to keep going. I am too invested in this, I have waited too long. I have been through all the drugs and the hormones, all the awful choices, and the thought of abandoning it is simply horrendous. It is too much for one person.

The phone call ends and I tell the carpenter what has

happened. He doesn't really have a lot to say about it, though he is sorry to find me upset. He says it is *my* decision. He says this, and yet he has clear opinions on what he does and doesn't want. He won't allow me certain options. So, really it's only a choice within the realms of his shortlist and therefore not a real choice... I know what he is doing. He thinks he is absolving himself of all responsibility for the choice that I make for both of us. He can then be free to hate me for it. He doesn't want any part in it, including being included. Including being a husband.

30th July

Here we are. The day of my final scan. The day of the injection. The point of no return.

Things have mercifully calmed down. I have seen the acupuncturist twice for more torture since I last spoke to the hospital. And, for once, I'm glad. It seems to have done the trick. The hospital is still on the fence but *I* am certain. We are *doing* this. There is too much lined up and I can't bear the thought of falling at this hurdle and having to unpick it all.

Some hours later, after numerous phone calls back and forth, they agree to go ahead. I take my epi-pen injection at exactly 7.30pm and have another session of acupuncture. There is no going back.

1st August

Today is a big day, and I've reached it with a certain amount of relief. We have made it to egg collection. I know the next bit is likely to be very hard but at least the first part is over, so I feel like I can stop holding my breath for a little while. We are a step nearer.

We get to the hospital as scheduled for 6.30am, put on our gowns with their signature split up the back, and wait in silence. He hasn't eaten, and neither have I. He seriously doesn't want to be here and he has no intention of hiding it. It makes me instantly stressed.

Several nurses come in and out demanding various samples, blood pressure tests and paperwork over the next hour or so until the anaesthetist finally comes round to see us both. The carpenter is having his sperm removed directly from the source with a fine needle, like a blood test, and only needs a local anaesthetic. I have to be put completely under. I am nervous of hospitals, of the very smell of them, but the anaesthetist puts me at my ease. He has a kind, unruffled way about him and a lovely winning smile.

The carpenter is taken for his procedure and, once they bring him back and perk him up with tea and toast, they take me down to theatre, the nurses talking to me as we walk, keeping things light and breezy.

I lie down as instructed on the theatre bed feeling quite calm. Then, suddenly, the nice anaesthetist, ready to pump me full of the sleep-inducing drugs, catches me off guard and tries to inject me right into the crook of my arm rather than in the back of my hand where I was expecting it. My reaction is severe, frightened and totally subconscious. I have flashbacks to Leeds Royal Infirmary all those years ago, where they tried to pin me down.

I freak out, pulling my arm out of his grasp, pushing at him with my feet saying, 'No, no, no, no, please, *please* don't!' I don't want anyone touching my skin with any more needles, especially *there*, I can't stand it.

They try to be professionally firm and hold my arm in place but I can feel the panic rising in my chest as I twist about on the table trying to free myself. I've been stuck with so many pins recently that it's made me emotional and jumpy. I *know* how much it hurts and my phobia resurfaces. I am beyond panicked. The tears come quickly. They are fiercely hot and desperate, burning my face, spewing and vomiting my tattered little heart out of them. The reality of all that has happened to me, where I am, what we are doing, what we are *not* doing, how very alone and frightened I feel and what I'm left with of my husband and marriage is right there in front of me, right there in those tears.

I can't stop them coming. The poor anaesthetist looks annoyed with me to begin with, but his expression quickly changes to utterly mortified as he sees how beside myself I am. He puts the needle down and strokes my arm, my hair, and I wish in that moment I had a husband like him. One who would guard me, soothe me and not abandon me to all this.

I calm down, and before I know it, the anaesthetist has expertly slipped the line and the drugs into the back of my hand and the room ghosts, swims, becoming unfocused – and suddenly I am awake again, an hour later, with only stained cheeks to show for my sorry episode.

A few hours later, the carpenter's mate picks us up. He doesn't talk much and neither do we. The hospital said the sperm were much better this time and that we achieved a harvest of 25 eggs. I distinctly dislike that word now: *Harvest*. I feel like an inanimate object when they say it, as if I am some sort of farmable field, rather than a living, breathing, feeling person. But we should have a good round, which I am happy about.

We get home and I wait for the inevitable pain – once they've taken your eggs, all those follicles start filling and draining with fluid. When it comes, it is far worse than the last time. They said it would be. They no longer think

I'm going to require hospitalisation but I'm not out of the woods entirely and my ovaries are 'busy'. They are still floating around as they please, and I can feel them, boulder-sized, lodging themselves in strange places, the pain going absolutely everywhere.

My specialist has still insisted that if I am unwell over the weekend then they *will* freeze the entire batch of embryos and do a transfer another time. Falling pregnant with OHSS can be very dangerous as pregnancy pushes your hormone readings up further still. I can accept this, because at least we didn't have to totally abandon it all and, once the embryos are 'made', there won't really be any excuse that the carpenter can create to not use them up.

But right now all I can do is lie here. Ironically, I look like I'm expecting.

4th August

I'm in too much pain. It has been an awful few days. My poor swollen belly is as tight as a balloon and my ovaries have wedged themselves behind my bladder. Every time I have to pee I can feel them crashing downwards when I've finished. The pain of it is exquisite, astonishing even, a searing pain that flashes through my belly, making me scream as I let my water out. The carpenter even came into the bathroom to hold my hand, so primeval was the noise I was making, and I squeezed the very life out of him, swearing loudly. I'm sure the neighbours think he's beating me up or that we're into some serious BDSM. Perhaps I should send a note round to reassure them.

At 10.30am, the hospital phones with news of our growing embryos. Seventeen out of the 25 eggs they found have fertilised, but one has arrested overnight, leaving 16.

Everyone is pleased with this positive result. Things are much better than last time and I tell the carpenter that I am proud of him for taking the recommended supplements and curbing the drinking. He doesn't say much.

They say that as of today we have several early blastocysts and the others are all high-grade eight-cell embryos, so we can leave the embryo transfer until Monday, which they recommend. Over the weekend the unlikely candidates, the ones that don't have the capability of creating a full embryo, will die off, leaving only the strongest ones to carry on. There is the small chance that nothing will survive the next few days, of course, but the hospital believe, especially given our good numbers, that this is unlikely to happen. And I am *so relieved*. Not only because we *have* embryos, but also because we have the coveted *blastocyst!* This means that, all being well, we'll be transferring a five-day-old blastocyst after the weekend, which is much more likely to continue growing and go on to produce a pregnancy and, fingers crossed, a live baby. It also means my body can recover some more. I doubt whether I could have had a transfer today even if it had been necessary, we'd have had to freeze everything instead, so I am thrilled we're still on course.

The fact that we can keep going as planned pleases the carpenter too. He much prefers the immediacy of this, hoping that it will soon be over, decided one way or the other and that it won't drag on. He gives me a little cuddle before going to get on with some DIY in the stepson's room.

The stepson comes down and we watch a film together. He keeps me topped up with water so I don't have to get up more than I need to. He is such a nice young man: kind, considerate – so very different from his father in a great many ways. He becomes engrossed in the film, but my mind wanders as it endlessly does these days. I do not let it take me under the water today. I do not want to see the gnarled face of the carpenter as he reaches menacingly for our child. I watch the palm tree in the front garden instead, dancing around in the breeze as I breathe through the pain, wishing the time away.

5th August

The pain is still with me though it doesn't quite reach the same heights, despite the continuing heat doing its best to add to my discomfort.

It is *unbearably* hot. I lay flat out on the sofa, sweating endlessly, consuming ice lollies by the box, just to try to stay cool. And with every rocket lolly, every Twister that I consume, my mind churns great multitudes of information around and around. I am armed with so many facts that I almost wish for blissful ignorance and blind faith. 'Informed thinking' is my latest form of torture, and I can't turn this white noise off.

I pray things will be all right to go ahead tomorrow, that our embryos make it through the weekend and there will be lots of choice with some good ones to freeze. The 'some to freeze' part is still so very important and worrying for me. Because I don't want it to be over – not until age takes me to 'too late'. I don't want to be anywhere near having to accept childlessness. I want that potential future to be a long way off, somewhere far in the future where I can hardly see it.

I try to relax and think positive thoughts. I imagine them, our tiny embryos, each in their own little petri dish somewhere in the depths of the hospital, growing, multiplying. I think beyond eight-cell clusters and blastocysts, to real live babies and what it might be like giving birth. I realise how much I will welcome the blinding pain of it. I try to imagine the tone of our baby's first cry, to taste knowing that my child is finally here, alive and breathing, making his shrill fanfare. I collate a mental list of names, visualising the nameplate on the nursery door that the carpenter will make for their first birthday. I love the name Austin for a boy, Maddison for a girl. I like unusual names. The carpenter does too. *This* we agree on.

I've been looking through the Next catalogue all day at nursery furniture. It is *so* lovely. I try to plan out the baby bedroom that we might create and once I have it in my mind's eye I turn to the carpenter, who is stretched out on the other sofa, and tell him my ideas. He smiles at me, nodding, agreeing. I smile back. I feel lifted at this and I chatter away, letting myself enjoy this little bit of excitement that I would normally keep hidden under a tight lid, allowing tiny bubbles of happiness to effervesce over.

I realise I'm getting a touch carried away, and stop momentarily, but my abrupt halt does not register with him. He is still nodding away, smiling at me and I suddenly wonder if he's got more than half an eye on the football. I peer, trying to work out if he's really tuned into what I'm saying, or if he is just pacifying me. When someone scores, it turns out to be the latter and I get up, deflated (in only the metaphorical sense, sadly) to get more fluids. I roll off the sofa with all the grace of a beached sea cow and potter through to the kitchen.

I sigh as I open the fridge. I'm hoping for apple juice. I'm sick to the back teeth of water, but there are only a few drops left in the carton: a small disappointment but annoying nonetheless. I throw the empty carton away, irritated with the boys for putting it back in there. Why do they put empty cartons back in the fridge? *Almost* empty bottles? If it's only got a dribble in it, and I mean *a dribble*, surely it's time to recycle it? And it's not just cartons, it can apply to containers of any sort. The other week I was looking for mushrooms, and there, in their place, was the empty tray, devoid of all mushrooms. What is the explanation for this strange behaviour?

Disgruntled, I get some water and waddle back to where I came from. I gingerly set myself back down and turn the football over without asking. I'm fed up of being second to the damn magic box so I commandeer it, flicking through the channels. There's nothing on, but the hours are passing so slowly and I need to drown out my incessant inner radio. I break open my *Friends* DVD box set and put it on, starting at episode one.

6th August

It is Monday morning and the phone is ringing. I know it is the hospital and I am horribly nervous. I grab for the phone, losing it a couple of times as it jumps about in my fingers, before I can answer to my favourite nurse. We cut straight to the point, neither of us seeing any sense in faffing about or making small talk. She asks how I feel.

'Well enough to proceed,' I tell her, so she goes on.

'There's one good blastocyst to put back,' – the pause in her voice makes me panic – 'and we're still waiting to see on the others, but I'm not sure any of them will be suitable to freeze. I'm sorry.'

And there's that crash again. A massive wave of disappointment rushing over me, leaving all but the tiniest pocket of happiness rinsed clear.

She waits for me to answer but I don't.

I hardly breathe.

I *am* happy that we have an embryo for the transfer, of course I am, but I am all too aware that this could be the one and only remaining chance. And somehow my sinking heart breaks despite the good news.

The freezing is such a crucial thing for us, well, for *me*. Everyone thought that this time we'd cracked it, that we'd got a good strong batch. Yet here we are again. How have we gone from having loads to just having one good one? I'm distant as they book me in for a transfer at 2.30pm. They'll know more about the others then, they say.

I go off to the acupuncturist's for more relaxing pins. I pick the carpenter up from work on the way back, change and head over to the hospital.

When we arrive, we are ushered straight into theatre. I change out of my clothes from the waist down and into my 'modesty sheet', which really doesn't live up to its title. I am left to choose which part of myself to leave hanging out, before tiptoeing my way across the floor to the bed. Once again, the clinical environment makes me feel anxious.

The carpenter isn't saying anything, making his feelings perfectly clear, and it is embarrassing. The setting has brought it home to him again that this is all actually happening, no more playing along behind a curtain of detachment.

My modesty sheet is not helping. I am bare under here, I feel vulnerable and there is a hostility radiating from the carpenter as he sits by my side, letting me hold just two of his fingers as if he will catch some sort of hideous disease from me. I feel unwanted. I feel like a *thing*.

The nurse tells us again that there is one good one to put back, but still nothing to freeze at the moment. One has arrested altogether, the others are still compacting. But, she says, if we want to put *two* back then there are a few other early blastocysts to choose from. Maybe one of those, too?

I look at the carpenter hopefully, but am instantly put in my place.

'No, I'm only doing one, and that's it,' he spits out at the room, jarringly.

The nurses look at each other, a little taken aback, then break the tension with a flurry of movement, whipping my feet up into the slack, black stirrups before I can even let my heart knot itself.

I shouldn't feel upset or disappointed. Some women would kill to have gotten this far, to have even one blastocyst, to have anything at all! It's actually gone very well in that respect. It is the carpenter's negativity, and unreasonable attitude towards all this that is the true problem, and it is overwhelming. If we only put one back and the others don't make the grade, then they will all go down the drain, wasted. And the closer *I* will be to *never* being a mummy, because of him. The disappointment is for the future, and it is bitter. My knees are hanging open, I am totally exposed in every way a person can be, my face is red with embarrassment as I *half* hold the carpenter's hand, staring at the ceiling, too numb to even cry...

There are jokes being made about how flexible my hips are as I mentally return to the moment.

'You should've been a ballet dancer,' they jest.

I try to be jolly and chat along. I tell them that I do drama. I say I love to dance though I doubt I'd have been good enough to be a proper ballerina. He curls his top lip at this subject, so I shut up.

The nurses continue setting everything up, chatting among themselves to diffuse the angst in the air. I close my eyes and shrink into myself, going to that safe place inside my mind, remembering back to a time when the carpenter used to respect me and what I did, when he cared for me and protected me. He wanted to keep me safe. Once upon a time he was even chivalrous, as outdated as that is. He always said he'd do anything for me...

Then

It is a hot summer's night. We are in the kitchen at my house, the friends from Bangkok and I, washing up and making drinks, being silly, having fun. The carpenter has gone across the road to Londis to get some Coke so we can make Long Island Iced Teas. We are happy and life is simple. Their child is asleep in the spare bedroom and we are enjoying an evening of catching up.

We are dragged out of our conversation abruptly when we hear an awful thudding and crashing coming from the front room. We look to each other, confused, wondering what the hell has fallen over. We take breath to speak but are stopped when we hear the carpenter cry out.

For a moment I think he is pratting around, pretending to have fallen over in some sort of attempt to be comically theatrical. We then hear other strange muffled sounds, those of struggling and scuffling. It dawns on me that this is serious and I run through, expecting to see him flat out on the floor with a broken ankle.

For a moment, I stand there, my mouth agape. The carpenter is indeed in need of assistance. With him – or rather *on* him – is a huge man of unknown identity, and the two of them are wrestling each other on the living room floor. A million thoughts flash through my mind at breakneck pace as I stand, shocked and rooted to the spot.

There is a man in my living room? Oh my God, *there is a man in my living room*! An intruder! Has he attacked the carpenter on the way home? Has he followed him, pounced on him, mugging him on the way back? Has the carpenter dragged him all the way back, trying to get away, trying to get home?

Suddenly I realise that the carpenter still requires *actual* help. Without thinking, I run in and grab the unidentified man, furious that he has had the audacity to attack my partner and that he is doing so in my home! I grab him by the collar (how clichéd), and find that I am yelling at him, screaming in his face with frothy-mouthed outrage demanding to know what the hell he is doing in my house! The unidentified man looks absolutely bloody terrified, and so he should be. I'm wearing my scarlet face of fury and am beyond apoplectic.

'How dare you!' I roar, my brain adding the extra expletives that I am too livid to spit out. I signal to the carpenter that we should just get him out of the house and we throw open the door, tumbling out into the inky air. We try to hurl him back into the night from whence he came, just wanting to get him as far away as possible, but the carpenter trips, still holding onto the man's legs. The intruder's jeans, which are of the stupid baggy variety, complete with pants hanging out the back of them, are now round his knees. The brute kicks the carpenter off, then, flailing and panicking, he legs it, spluttering that he is sorry, pulling his trousers up as he trips and runs.

I continue to holler at him like a banshee, until the man is swallowed by the darkness and disappears out of the front gate. I turn to the carpenter and see that he has fallen onto his knees. My stomach churns, I go white. The way he has fallen, crumpled into a heap, he looks like he has been knifed in the belly and my heart is in my throat. I rush over and grab at him, asking if he is okay, over and over. He doesn't answer straight away and I shake him, repeating myself, becoming more frantic. Then suddenly he grabs hold of me tightly, his winded voice coming back to him, and he tells me he is all right.

Instant relief washes over me. He is not hurt. He's cut his

ankle open and his fingers a little too, but he's fine. I'm still shaking with fury and adrenalin. It's a strange mixture of emotions, to be so relieved and so violently angry all at once. But I am overwhelmingly grateful that it wasn't worse, grateful that my eyes deceived me and that the carpenter is unharmed.

He gathers himself and sits up strongly, smiling his crooked smile. I am still shaking but he wraps his big arms around me, soothing me a little. 'I just didn't want him getting *you*, darlin'.'

I smile, realising it's the only time he's ever called me that.

'I came back and he was just there in the house. I didn't want him to hurt you. Trust you to join in, babes!' We laugh nervously, both of us realising just how scared we were of the other getting hurt.

My friend has called the police and brings me the phone. She is terrified because someone broke in with her child in the house, and orders a group retreat. The child, miraculously, is still asleep, and we all pull back, locking ourselves firmly inside to await the local constabulary.

The carpenter tells us that Londis had been shut (I hadn't noticed the absence of a fit-to-explode Coke bottle rolling around the scene) and that he hadn't locked the door when he went out because we were all *in*. He said he came straight back to find the door ajar and on entering the living room found the man, already in there, leaning over the sofa attempting to steal the laptop. That was what the crash had been, the laptop hitting the deck! I couldn't believe it. The man had *actually* sneaked in and tried to steal stuff when we were all quite clearly *in*...

I impart all of this to the telephone handler, having given her an astonishingly good description of the man's underwear as the boys in blue arrive at the door.

We relay the story once again and the police are surprised that is wasn't worse. They send a squad car over to sweep the area, though they don't seem hopeful that he'll still be lurking anywhere. The rest of us have a sugary cup of tea. They say we are lucky, and we feel it. For a moment I really thought the worst had happened, and realise how terrified I was of losing the carpenter... It was *he* who was guarding *me*.

He keeps his arms around me as we talk to the police. I simmer down. I'm upset still and rather shocked, but he is steady and sure. I feel utterly protected. I believe he will always look after me.

6th August cont.

I snap back to reality as they prise me open and realise just how much has changed between the two of us since then.

I try to relax, I try to be Zen. I try to do what the acupuncturist has told me to, but this is nigh-on impossible given the situation. I'm supposed to take myself off to that place in my mind under the water, and let myself float away.

I feel the warmth of the sun on my skin. I see the sea, blue and beautiful. I see the steps of an ancient staircase made out of grey stone that leads into the warm water, continuing underneath it. I prepare. I start walking down the steps... 1...2...3...

A sharp tug inside drags me out of the mental water. I close my eyes. I try again.

I feel the warmth of the sun on my skin. I see the sea... blah, blah, blah.... ancient staircase... blah, blah, blah, warm water... yada, yada... I start walking down the steps... 1...2...3... I see the carpenter's face, crooked and twisted like a gnarled old tree, he takes a swipe at my water baby...

My stomach turns. I can't escape the now. They are sliding the catheter in and it feels as though someone is doing the washing-up in my uterus. I don't think the carpenter really knows what to do or say to make it any easier for either of us. He can hide nothing and neither can I. I feel defenceless, and somehow violated.

But it goes extremely well, I'm told. The doctor (a different one from last time) says she is very pleased with the procedure. I like her and I know she is being truthful.

She reminds me of my mum a little, or perhaps an older version of myself – to the point, but caring, focused and honest. Not that I didn't like the other guy, he was lovely. But when it's gone badly or hasn't worked out, you hope that this new person will do it for you, be your lucky charm, achieve the miracle. I hope that somehow fate has spoken, rearranging things for the better – and that in two weeks' time, I'll be able to say that it was meant to be.

They leave us for a few minutes afterwards, to let my insides settle. We say nothing. He stares at the ceiling. So do I. Then I carefully get off the bed and change, moving as smoothly as I possibly can so as not to disturb my precious cargo. We walk out of the hospital entrance and I pause and look at him in the sunlight, hoping that he'll kiss me and cuddle me like that other man did with his wife. But he just walks on ahead and says, 'Come on, I've got the car on a meter.'

8th August

I spend the next two days on the sofa dutifully resting, glued to the Olympics. I'm watching any and every sport, the timing is a godsend really. Without Beth Tweddle to root for and Jessica Ennis pegging it about my TV screen, I'm not sure I'd be able to distract myself suitably.

Despite the carpenter's U-turn and the atmosphere at home, I feel quietly excited for myself, like I'm the keeper of a big secret. I get up for nothing except to use the loo and to transfer myself between the bedroom and the couch. I do nothing that could disrupt the little life. I like knowing he is in there – no one can flush *him* down a sink. He is safe inside his mummy.

Like last time, I am using the awful vaginal pessaries,

the bullets of progesterone designed to support pregnancy. I've gone through more pairs of knickers in the last two days than I normally use in a week. These waxy horrors are the messiest things in existence and I have to insert one three times a day. It is disgustingly sticky and yet another indignity of the whole affair, though I'm trying to see the humorous side.

10th August

A couple of days later, when I've done my bed rest, the tiny embryo and I go for a gentle walk up to the job centre. I must continue to go to these dreadful appointments. When they eventually get round to me I squirm in the chair as they look over my limited attempts at finding work these last two weeks, just wishing I could go home and change my underwear.

There are no interviews for me, though with my return to work looming we're all just formally treading water until they can sign me off. So they release me with a weary sigh and I wander back to the house. I do some gentle chores – wash the dishes, kill off a few more of the ants that are busy destroying the fruit tree and try not to think about the little life too much.

14th August

I have pains inside me. They go down my legs, nagging, and I change rapidly from hot to cold. These are *new* pains, new sensations, and I go online, trawling the web for information to prove that they are a good sign. I'm hoping they are implantation pains. It's about the right time, I think, and I feel a nervous flutter of excitement butterfly in my chest.

I open up the Next catalogue again and look longingly at what we might buy. But this time I go a step further. I go up to the little bedroom at the back of the house, lay a hopeful palm on the handle, and carefully push open the door. I haven't allowed myself into this room since I spent days in here lovingly painting the walls in 'parfait', before sealing it up. I wanted to preserve the idea of what it represented, so I've left it undisturbed. I didn't want it to be tainted with negativity like the rest of the house. But now I breathe it in, the smell of its new carpet, as I get out the tape measure and mark out the floor, meticulously figuring out what will fit. I look up the dimensions of my favourite cot and map it out. I throw in a wardrobe, a nursing chair, shelves, books, bunting, curtains: I can visualise the whole nursery in my head. I see a blanket I like, too, and all sorts of little baskets to store things in. I might as well just ring up the Next warehouse, quote the page number, and say I'll take the lot.

The carpenter comes home tired and ratty for no particular reason and doesn't want to talk to a keyed-up hormonal woman about baby bedroom furniture. But I've been here all day on my own with no one to speak to, and I really want to talk to my husband because we might be having a baby and I am burning to get giddy about it but he simply won't let me.

So instead of talking about cots and car seats, I end up telling him that I'm very worried because of how he is feeling again, and his attitude towards me. I say I am worried that this baby will actually just rip us apart rather than cement our relationship, and that I'm scared because I think I'm effectively going to be a single mum. I tell him that I feel pushed away, that he is rejecting the idea of having our baby. And that it is the *ultimate* rejection. I blurt out all my pent-up angst trying to make him see that I need him, and that I don't mean just financially. I need him to help and look after me, *me* on the *inside*. I say that I need him to be kinder.

Once again he gives me his stock response, saying that I'm not to expect him to get excited about it but that he'll try his best. He cracks open a bottle of wine to celebrate this pledge – and I want to hit him over the head with it. I follow him out to the patio to try and get to the bottom of all of this, to expose the roots, once and for all. I want him to talk to me. I want him to let me in, let me help him. I tell him I will listen to him, that I want to understand where it's all coming from.

He says if I understood, I'd never ask him to have a baby. My frustration begins to mount as I remind him, once again, that I have assumed nothing. And besides, most people do go on to be parents, I say. It is in our natural make-up, our animalistic instinct. Women are designed to bear children – it's part of life's progression. Thinking I may eventually go off the idea is an odd concept. It's more normal to have kids than to not...

But he has stopped listening. He is staring straight ahead, ignoring me. I am upset and I don't want to let it go, not this time. I want to *deal* with it. But I know I have to remain calm, not that I want to right now. Right now I want to yell at him and hurl the wine down the garden.

Instead I go back inside and watch more of the Olympics, putting the Next catalogue to one side as Beth Tweddle takes to the bars.

15th August

After the weekend, I can bear the waiting no longer. I must test. I have the pretty pink tests this time, which, ridiculously, makes me feel more hopeful.

I pee. I close the lid on the test and set it on the edge of the bath. I wait. I stare at the ceiling for a while, then out of the window, then at myself in the mirror, wondering when I got all those laughter lines...

One minute.

I pace up and down, as far as a person can in a bathroom, then clean the sink for want of anything else to do – all the while trying not to look at the little pink stick. It is torturous. The minutes are so very long. Why can't they be like minutes on the underground? They're always much quicker.

Two minutes.

I take a deep breath and approach the test. And there it is. A double pink line. It is faint, but it is there.

I feel giddy. I laugh nervously to myself, smiling broadly. It is the best feeling in the world. I stand and stare at the test in case it changes for some reason, but no, it is true.

I don't call to tell him. Not yet. I don't want to jinx it. He is trying to be better like he promised. He's not trying very *hard*, but he *is* trying.

My little life is trying too. I feel like it is *mine* rather than ours. How can it feel like it's ours when its daddy doesn't really want it?

I spend the day watching episodes of *One Born Every Minute* back to back. I mentally note some tips but I turn it off quickly when the carpenter's key turns in the lock. He *hates* this programme.

I am happy that he is home though. I'm dying to tell him about my little pink line, but I know that it's way too early to be sure and I have no real idea how he'll take it, so for now I keep it protected. My safe, happy, smile of a fragile little secret.

The carpenter must've had a good day today, or maybe it is part of his 'trying harder', because tonight we cuddle on the sofa. We watch *Coronation Street* like usual and I feel a little more contented than I have in a while.

We go to bed early. I struggle to drop off but, when I do, I dream of bumps. I am hugely pregnant in the dream, my belly massively swollen as I lie on a bed waiting to give birth. There are nurses all around me telling me to push, but suddenly I sit up and the bump has gone. I panic, my splayed fingers reaching under the covers, raking over every inch of cotton, looking everywhere in the bed for a baby. But all I find is a sleeping carpenter before I realise that it was just a dream.

16th August

I resist testing again. I try to push myself through the whole day by doing the mundane: the washing, the cleaning, the ironing. I take a little walk. I talk to my best friend on the phone, both of us skirting around the issue.

By lunchtime, I give in and test again. I want to see that little pink line getting stronger. I go through the same rigmarole as before while the test is busy testing, leaving the bathroom gleaming, but when I look back to it, the line is not there.

I think it must be wrong, it must be a duff. I fumble and rip open another packet, quickly squeezing a few more drops out onto the stick, but two minutes later there is still nothing. I hurriedly guzzle water from the tap and wait impatiently for an hour before doing another test. I continue like this for hours doing another, then another, and another until the day is almost spent with drinking, peeing and waiting. But the extra line has gone away, it is simply not there. I look at the tests and the open packets around me, like a strange binge gone wrong. I feel hollow.

That night we bicker and argue about every little thing a couple possibly can. He is snappy about how little I've done around the house and I'm resentful for being made to feel like the staff, as if all I'm here for is to clean up after everyone else. The carpenter is even nasty with the stepson, who is trying very hard to pull his weight. He is making a family lasagne alongside his father, who is slicing tomatoes with venomous, full-fisted chops as if he were logging. I wish the carpenter were in a better mood. Tonight I would have loved cuddles on the sofa again as I feel so forlorn, but it seems that all I can look forward to is sitting around the dining table eating lasagne in silence as the carpenter sinks another bottle. Things used to be so different.

Then

I step out into a wall of heat, leaving the cool air-conditioned office behind me for another day. Simply too warm to even contemplate taking the tube, never having been a fan of nose-to-armpit cosiness at the best of times, I slowly walk down to the main line through the park, enjoying the late afternoon sun.

It has been quiet in the office this summer – although I rather suspect we're in the eye of the storm. It never stays quiet for long, and that's the way I like it. But while I love the thrill and bustle of my office and its busy little bubble, I don't want these lazy summer days to end. The carpenter and I are happy with our sleepy post-work routine. He gets home early and fires up the barbecue, and I arrive back later, feeling unusually relaxed, to a jug of something refreshing and spicy fish kebabs.

He smiles as he organises everything, slowly smothering king prawns in garlic and chilli oil before throwing them on the grill. I pour a drink and close my eyes as the cooking smells, and now-bearable heat, make my eyelids heavy. He kisses me on the cheek between batches; I put my feet up on the chair opposite and look out at our pretty garden. The patio is looking lovely, it's all finished now, with great sprays of brilliant red flowers sprouting from every container pot. They make a nice contrast to the group of green parakeets that has decided to grace our garden and its little piece of sky. Sitting out here is simply the perfect end to the day. All feels balanced. Calm. Easy. The carpenter and I don't even need to talk. Often we just sit lost in our own thoughts as the little flashes of green dart across the sky, slowly becoming silhouettes as the light fades.

The line has definitely gone. It is two days since the day of testing and the family lasagne. I am at the end of the longest two-week wait in the world. The pains that came and went, the possible implantation pains, have started again and my feet are burning for some reason. I worry that the little life has given up, that maybe I killed him with the stress of our arguing. I feel sick, weak. The carpenter does seem concerned that I'm feeling unwell and I make the mistake of telling him that I've tested negative. I blurt it out, desperate for his support.

'Well, maybe it's not meant to be,' he says. 'Maybe you're just not meant to be a mum. I don't really understand why you *want* a kid anyway, babes.' His manner is flippant, barely concealed happiness at the prospect of not having to be a parent again.

He is pleased. He thinks he has got away with it. I am crushed. His words mark me, hurting me furiously. I catch sight of myself in the mirror and see I have flushed red all over.

'How can you say that?' I almost plead. I am not supposed to be getting worked up of course, even though I fear it is all but over anyway, but the rage inside me boils over as I finally let go of myself, yelling at him through bared teeth, with burning wet eyes. 'How can you act as if you couldn't care less? I am so sick and tired of this f-ing behaviour, this blowing hot and cold! I can't cope with it any more; I can't cope with *you* any more. I don't even see that we have a future! *How can you do this to me?*' I tell him it is like torture, that he is being cruel. I ask what he thinks will happen when I have to go back to work. Does he think that he won't have to do his share? Read to our child? Do bath times? That it'll all be me forever more?

He goes off on a strange rambling tangent, telling me that he thinks my parents should relocate to the south so they can be here to help out, if we all want a baby in the family so badly. I tell him that I think he is a deranged, ludicrous man.

'You can't ask people to relocate because *we* have a child, and *you* can't be arsed. That's preposterous! And besides, your mother lives round the corner!' I tell him we'll have to manage between us. Having a baby gives us *both* responsibility, *both* a duty of care: him *and* me. The duties do not fall down solely in one camp or the other and are certainly not the responsibility of our parents. It is a shared experience. I say I do not want to have a baby with someone who doesn't want to have one. I have been desperate to say that for so long. I am excruciatingly angry. 'If all I wanted in life was to have a baby then I could just go out and get knocked up!' I say. 'Loads of people do *that*! But that's not what I've ever wanted. I want *a family*. I want to see my baby's daddy sweep his little one up into his arms – smiling, holding it aloft, loving it, *wanting* it, caring and investing in it.'

The carpenter screams back in my face as I cry, the same things he always has. He says that if I were him I wouldn't want to do it either. He says that his friends think he's mad, and practically godlike for even *considering* doing it all again, and that they actually don't understand why *any* women would want to work *and* be a mum. (I want to throttle his friends!) He asks me why I want a baby and, more crucially, why I'd want to have a baby and then go back to work and leave it. He tells me that if I want to be a mum so badly then it should be enough for me full stop. He adds that his mother agrees and thinks I should give up my career entirely if I want to have children: that it is the sacrifice a woman should make. Why should *he* have to pick up the slack?

I am verging on hysteria as I ask what era his friends and family are living in. I am shocked. Repulsed. Dizzy. I do *not* feel well. The truth of his beliefs has come pouring out and I see our future engulfed in flames and lies. I put my hand to my hot head, trying to catch my breath and balance, but the upset gets the better of me, ripples up my throat, and I throw up. I do not get to the sink in time. He stops in his tracks and comes to helps me. But I don't want his help. I don't want him *near* me right now. I am beside myself. Affronted. Offended. I push him away and clean up the sick.

He opens a bottle of wine.

Later...

Night time. It is almost pitch black in the house. Delicately I feel for the stairs beneath my feet, running my fingers along the smooth, newly plastered wall, sensing my way downstairs. I put on the light and find my notepad and take out a nice sharp new pencil. And I begin – a long heart-pouring letter, as if I am writing the pain into the pages so it can't hurt me any more. I feel I'm transferring it, putting it away somewhere, to be looked at, read, but not lived everyday. I always write in pencil at times like these. It is more immediate somehow, I can write more quickly. Perhaps I like it because the words can be rubbed away afterwards if I want, taking the pain with them.

I have always wanted to be a mum. Not *just* a mum

though, I wanted a good career as well, something for me, something I worked hard for. I wanted a marriage too.

From the age of about seven, I remember looking longingly at all the little baby clothes in Asda, where we did our weekly food shop. I wanted to buy and dress my Cabbage Patch Kid in them, because I knew you weren't allowed babies until you were much older. Even in high school, when all I thought about was boys, I knew it wasn't acceptable to push a pram through the school gates so, of course, I waited, like any sensible young lady. I waited until the time when you were *allowed*. All the while, I worked hard at school, I gained my degree at university and found my way into a wonderful career. I forged it over years and grafted away at it and I do *not* want to give it up.

I locked away my little baby dream safely in a box, and tucked it up in the back of my mind for the day when someone would come along who loved me enough, someone who I would spend my life with. I saved it for a time when I was ready and it was *allowed*. Even with my first husband I didn't feel like it was. We'd been married for eight years, but had no baby. We were young when we got together and we just hadn't got round to it, I suppose. When the marraige fell apart I was devastated. We were so close to having everything, and then it was gone. I didn't want to go back to the beginning again, not when I felt I'd finally made it. But I had to and I did.

Then again, its not like I've been sitting around getting hysterical about it all these years, crying into my soup, not at all. I had my career, my other love and drive, the other thing that holds me. But the void is still there. You can't put a square peg in a round hole after all.

Pets have been a good sticking plaster as well. They've come and gone as the years have gone by. As a kid there was my beloved cat Peardrop who was beautiful and loved me to death. Indeed she would bring me death in the form of mangled love-offerings on a regular basis. She vanished one day. I went away to university and I got a phone call from home to say she hadn't come home. I knew that I wouldn't see her again.

Poppy, my darling ex-dog from my ex-marriage, certainly went a long way to assuaging the strange loneliness that has always been there. I loved and treated her – minus dressing her up in silly dog clothes – as if she were a child. And even when it was all over with the ex and I had to send her up to Leeds because I couldn't manage her on my own, she was still *my* dog and I still felt hope. I was starting a new life. All the possibilities lay before me again. I wanted to find a good husband, one who I adored, who really valued me, one who wanted a family one day: someone who would *allow* it. And I thought I'd found it in the carpenter.

The loneliness comes back to me night after night as I lie awake, hot and sweaty, with my feet burning and my arms freezing. I wait, knowing already that it is probably over, wondering once again how I will live if I never experience the feeling of a little life growing inside me. Will I carry this sadness around with me always? It has been such a journey to this point and I don't honestly know if I have any more energy in me. I wonder what I did wrong?

There is still a scrap of hope: there is still the official test tomorrow. But I wonder if this scrap (and it really is a *scrap*) is something I allow myself to feel to ease the blow and let myself down gently with: to pace the grief and the tears out so they don't hit me in one great thud.

I wonder if I will ever get my happily ever after – but then again, what is happily ever after anyway? The perfect house? The perfect husband? The perfect dog and the perfect children who grow up to be, well... perfect? A life that looks as if Mary Poppins herself has been in and made magic a suburban reality? Who knows what perfect is anyway. Perfect for one person might be another person's hell. Perfect people – are they *really* perfect? Maybe they just *seem* perfect on the outside: perfect clothes and perfectly immaculate hair. Perhaps they are all perfectly bored? I find that my house is at its most perfect when I'm at my most fed up or lonely and I've simply been filling up my time cleaning like a crazy woman. Perfect comes as a result of imperfect. Maybe perfect doesn't even exist? And yet we place so much importance on it.

'My wedding has to be perfect.'

'I don't want to go out with him, he's not right for me. His eyebrows / dress sense / knife-holding isn't perfect.'

I wonder how many of the decisions we make are based on whether or not something is or isn't perfect. For example, a number of days ago I turned down one piece of cake in favour of another because it wasn't as evenly sliced. What if we all went around rejecting things simply because they were wonky? Maybe that's why there are so many one-eyed, gangly mutts in Battersea Dogs Home. My best friend rejected her pre-chosen Chihuahua puppy because his hair turned out to be a bit too long. He wasn't her idea of perfect and she swapped him, *after* she'd taken him home! He was flawed so back he went, poor little chap.

Perhaps I shall make a conscious decision to pick the imperfect things in life from now on: the ugly puppy with long hair, or no hair, the wonky piece of cake, the un-cool car.

Suddenly, I wonder: is this what I did with the carpenter?

19th August

The stepson finds me in the morning, asleep at the table. I go back upstairs. There is a letter waiting for me on the bed, from the carpenter, his first letter to me. It looks long. I leave it for now. Instead I go to the bathroom. I take out my little pink friends.

I test. I wait. One minute. Two minutes.

It is true; it is over.

I go back downstairs, pausing at the bottom of the steps. The postman puts some letters through the door. I open one that is addressed to me, my mind blank. It is a notice from the hospital of an unpaid IVF bill. The tears come again but I make no sound. They just roll down my face, very slowly, as if they, like me, are suddenly muted, on a slow play.

I think the bill must be a mistake. I've paid every bill on time. In any event, the timing of it landing on the doormat is unfortunate at best. We might as well have burnt the money.

I go through to the kitchen, tears dripping off my chin. He doesn't notice. He is making a tea. I go to the sink to get some water. I can't see for the tears. I try to keep quiet. I look out into the garden at the pear tree. I love the pear tree. I had hoped to put a swing in it one day.

I find a glass on the side and try to turn the tap on but my wrist is limp. I have no strength. I can't breathe. I bend over the stainless steel, trying to hold myself up. But I lose the fight with my legs and I slip down the unit to the floor, dropping the glass, landing crumpled on the floor like a used towel, my face pressed against the cupboard door.

The glass smashing is what grabs his attention. He asks me what is wrong but I cannot say the words. I can only gulp like a dying fish. He looks worried. He looks upset. I still cannot say that I've lost my little life, that it's gone, or whatever you're supposed to categorise it as. To me it has died. It takes an age to get the words out.

'I'm never going to be a mummy, am I?'

He kneels down by me and puts his arms through mine. He is with me again. I feel a fragment of support, a connection, finally. It is the support I've needed all along. His. No one else's.

He says that we'll try again, we'll adopt.

I say I don't want to adopt but also that I don't want him to make promises he has no intention of keeping.

He says we'll put more back, he promises. It is the only thing I want to hear and I have no choice but to believe him. He props me up. I am shaken, beaten, desolate. This pain is beyond compare.

He puts me to bed. I stop using the pessaries, they are holding off the inevitable. I lie and stare, the tears still rolling down my face. The blood comes quickly, later that same day.

Some hours later I ring the hospital. The nurses are very upset for me. I can barely speak but when I do my voice is faint and far away, as if it is detached from me. I tell them that he's said we can have another go. They schedule an appointment for a follow-up in a week or two. I am exhausted by the thought of this future attempt just as much as I am by this last one. I sleep.

23rd August

We go to Broadstairs – us, and a wide range of leathery-skinned people, many sporting tattoos and beer bellies which are, at least, a distraction...

As we pull up to the coast I lower my window. The scene beneath us sounds like a cocktail party, a loud cacophony of sound. On my first attempt to swim, once we've actually parked the car and made it down to the beach, I find I can't cope with the noise.

I've been silent for almost five days.

On my first day of silence, the carpenter took hold of me by my shoulders and shook me. He didn't do it violently. I think he was scared. It was as if he was trying to shake the words out of me. He thinks forcing me to speak will make it better. It doesn't. It makes it worse. I retreat further into myself, away from him, away from all the things that have hurt me. It is not fully a choice. The words are stuck whether I want them to be or not, and the more he shakes and shouts, the more lodged they become. They don't even reach my throat. If I could speak with my hands I could tell him *why* at least. How being mute is my only remaining defence, how my mind is protecting me from further invasion by refusing the world communication with me. It brings blissful relief. I don't have to let him in this way. It is something akin, perhaps, to a dirty protest made by child – they too have no power, no other way of showing their pain, frustration, anger. But I don't choose this, *it* chooses *me,* and I choose to go along with it. When I am silent, I do not partake in life like everyone else does. I have my own terms and conditions, my own rules. There will be no arguments, no bargaining, no reasoning, no words, no talking or trying. No tears. It is peaceful. Like in the water.

If I could talk with my hands, I'm not sure I would ever speak again. I am more sensitive than people realise, so fragile on the inside, despite my outward appearance. But I am safe when I am silent. No one can hurt me when I am in my mind. They can't hear it, or see what it is saying, feeling or commenting on. It is the only part of me that cannot be violated. It is mine and mine alone.

When the silence breaks it is almost painful for me. I walk down to the shoreline, tiptoeing across the sharp bits of washed-up shale, ready to feel the water round my feet. There are a few enormous youths splashing one another and I find that the timid part of myself, the vulnerable hurt girl that I am right now, can't bring herself to wade past them. I know I am being silly but their erratic movement is unnerving. I try again a bit further up the beach from them, wading in slowly. It is not all that warm, the water, but I look forward to the numbness it will ultimately bring. The pain of it is somehow enjoyable. I manage to swim for five minutes or so before the crowds start to get to me and I head back up to the sand.

I feel safer on the sand rather than in the sea, on account of all the people and their noise, but I crave my usual ocean fix. I want to swim, but it is too busy. I close my eyes, lie back on my towel. The air is warm and smells of salt. If I let myself drift off under the sun (provided the seagulls don't crap on me) I could almost be away on holiday. I pretend that we are. I need a holiday.

There is some sort of commotion and we sit up to find a woman in tears, frantically asking if we have seen her child. She is panic-stricken, clearly terrified that he's been taken, and as everyone tries to find the boy it causes a fleeting stab of my own loss that is as much a part of me now as my desire to have a child. She finally finds him wandering along the wrong line of windbreaks and drags him back to her own camp by the arm, telling him off as they both cry.

The carpenter goes for ice cream, but only comes back with one. He says I didn't say I wanted one. I pretend I don't mind. I last another half an hour on the beach before I start to get overwhelmed, and we wander up to the bustling promenade, retreating into the nearest chippy. We both love fresh scampi and he says he's sure we'll get some good ones here today. He rubs his hands together, smiling.

He is being nice today, lovely even. Though I am aware he is here more for himself than he is for me. He orders on my behalf. I may have broken my silence, but only just. I can't speak to other people. Not even chip shop owners. Especially not my friends and family. I don't want to have to say the disappointing words. I can't admit that this is, in fact, my actual life. Saying it seems so final.

The carpenter smacks his lips together to articulate the irrefutable sucess of his scampi dinner. He is making a purposeful show of being happy. I am quietly pretending. And while the sea, sun and salt do me good, I need more. I need more space and change. I need to feel better.

25th August

My favourite work friend and her husband come over. I speak to them. I open my mouth and say words. I stretch the truth and say that we're all okay, the carpenter and me, and that we're going to try again.

They are understanding. They've never really liked him and they don't trust him, but they do their best to be friendly in spite of everything. They make me laugh. It is such a relief to laugh. They leave me feeling happier. I have missed them. Like so many of my friends, I have barely seen them recently.

27th August

I am getting myself back together. At least I am doing

things. At some point in the day, I get up. I eat *some* food. I have started to plan family meals. The stepson is at home again, having made himself scarce during the awfulness of everything, favouring his mother's house for a while. I feel good about the meals. It is something I can control.

I do other jobs too, physical ones, which always helps. Today, I sanded the garden table, which didn't go terribly well. I then painted it two different shades of 'oak', neither of which I liked. Both looked orange. I sprayed the pear tree and both plum trees with some sort of scab killer for their various fruit tree diseases. They are more trouble then they're worth the carpenter says, claiming he's going to dig them up (I'd like to see him try, the pear tree is enormous!) so I'm trying to resurrect them. I won't let him kill anything else off that I love. I fell off the ladder doing it, landing quite badly among the rotted fruit on the grass. Not one neighbour or even my husband, who watched it happen from the kitchen window, came to help me. But I picked myself up anyway and carried on.

Even the fall hasn't jolted me out of the numbness that won't really be gone.

I also finally cleaned the utility room. Nothing had been working to get the filth off the walls, so I resorted to using washing powder. It turns out that the colour of the walls is actually lime green, not the strange shade of sage they've been masquerading as. I *hate* this rickety room, but at least, for now, it is finally sparkling and sanitary, if not a little on the bright side.

I make a plan to go up to my mother's for a few days. I think everyone hopes it will help and I shall return transformed back into my old self. But I know it will only be a change of scene. After all, there is nothing much to say about it all: it is what it is. At least when I had just a bad marriage to deal with I could choose to change it and start again. With that, there were things I could discuss with people. With this, *nothing* will change, no matter how much airtime I give it. The only thing that will change it is the very thing that evades us. If our treatment never works then I will *always* be childless, and perhaps some people have a very nice life, thank you very much, without children. A good life. But it is a different one.

The carpenter isn't enough on his own I've realised, not any more. I am drifting, coasting through the days. It's as if life can't really get going again. What will my lot, *our lot*, be? Will it just be him and me? The more I think about it, the more I realise I don't want it to be...

28th August

It is over a week since it happened. There is a knock at the door, which I hope isn't the Jehovah's Witnesses again. They won't stop calling by. They see a sad little woman and they want to help, but I don't know them or their God and I want them to leave me alone. Thankfully, it is just a man trying to sell double-glazing and I tell him that we've just had ours done. I close the door just relieved that he wasn't trying to sell me Jesus. The days have been so blurry. I have nothing to do. Nowhere I'm expected or needed, not yet, so I have to create jobs. Perhaps I should get back to some DIY?

30th August

We go to our follow-up appointment as scheduled. Sitting outside in the waiting room I notice a couple I've seen a few times. I wonder if they have happy or sad news? She looks very happy. We're not quite so cosy. We've been rather snappy with each other. I am keen to be cosy too, so I take hold of my husband's arm but he doesn't lift it up to put it round me. He reaches for a paper instead and flicks through the day's events until the nurse calls us in with the obligatory sympathetic head tilt.

'It didn't work,' the specialist declares as we enter the room. I'm not sure if he's asking a question or making a statement, but either way I have no words. I am still so upset. The specialist says we *must* put more than one embryo back. I look across at the carpenter to gauge his feeling on this. He's already said we can do this so I'm just looking for some sort of confirmation, his willing nod that says he's standing by me. But he is dead behind the eyes again and I just can't believe it. Or rather I can't believe I believed him. What an idiot I am. I give up. It seems his alter ego is back with us and I'm not even sure which one is the real him any more. His hatred of doing all this is tangible. He couldn't hide it if he tried.

We talk briefly, the three of us. It is awkward and stilted. The carpenter is quite clear that he won't risk having twins, and says no to putting more than one embryo back. I feel betrayed. I don't know whether I'm coming or going and any last fragments of trust I had in him evaporate.

The specialist tells him that we need to be flexible and give him more to work with, that we *have* to try something different now. Putting two embryos back gives us a better chance – but even then, still only a 40% chance of just *one* baby. He emphasises this point, trying to impress it upon us.

The mood feels heavy. I can sense the old demons. They sit in between us, mocking me as my torment creeps back in. The specialist sends us away with a tentative set of new dates and a piece of advice. He tells us, without taking his eyes off the carpenter, that we need to go away and decide whether or not we want to have a child, and then confirm with the nurses. My heart hangs heavily as we go through the door and into the waiting room that I know so well.

We get home. He hits the bottle. I watch the telly for half an hour or so to let the dust settle. When I go through to the dining room to try and talk about what happened he is already at the end of the bottle and starting the next one.

I ask him why he said we'd try again, put more back, when it's clear he doesn't mean it.

'I just said it to stop you crying,' he slurs.

I go white. Or at least I think I do.

'You said it to *stop me crying*?' I can't quite believe my ears. I ask him what sort of person does that, who says *that* knowing full well they don't mean it? Did he think the issue would never come up again or that at no point would I expect him to be true to his word? He *lied*. I ask him why he ever pursued me to begin with, *knowing* he never wanted to do be a dad again.

'I wanted to go out with you,' he says, gesticulating with the wine glass. 'So, you know, I just said...' and he shrugs. Neither of us needs to finish that sentence.

The argument escalates quickly, gaining momentum faster than any we've had before. He gets up from his seat and comes towards me, getting louder all the time. He says that *none* of this is about him. It's all about *me* and that I want it for *myself*. He says that I'm selfish, that I don't care about him, that if I loved him enough I wouldn't want or need to do any of this. He says that I love the idea of having a baby more than I love him!

His words are like fistfuls of ice, cold and sharp. And he is wrong, although the truth of how little love I have left for him smacks me squarely in the face. Who wants to have a baby under these circumstances?

'You just want it all your own way,' he spits, jabbing at me with a finger raised from the glass, sloshing the drink everywhere in the process.

'My way?' I reply. 'This is *no one's* way. It's not exactly anyone's dream option is it? *My* way would be with a husband who actually wants to do it and is prepared to be a good dad whether he's thrilled about it or not. Of all the ways I ever wanted to do this huge, normal thing that I have looked forward to for years, *this is not it!*'

I turn around and pace, pressing my hands to my face. How can he be doing this to me, again? How am I *still* putting up with it? I stand silently, my head in my hands. No one speaks for a few minutes. He is so different from the man I met. How could he tell me those lovely lies, then try to fob me off? Marry me knowing full well how he truly felt all along, knowing what I'd always wanted one day? Not a baby, but a *family*. What so many men and women want together. How could he expect me now to simply say, okay, let's not bother then, it's no big deal?

He speaks again. He doesn't yell this time but tries a different approach, snaking into another version of himself that has a new, altogether more dangerous dimension. He tries to 'sell me' an alternative version of life, claiming there will be lots of things we will never do if there are kids around. He puts a drunken arm around my shoulder and tries to sell me *holidays* as if they are the same thing as having a family, as if sunsets are the same as seeing your baby smile for the first time. I know that he is working every angle. His demeanour is cunning. He is secretly hoping I'll just give in. That he can talk me out of it.

He won't succeed, for I *see* him now, and what he is doing. It is all so very transparent. If you *can't* have a baby with someone, then it is sad, and it is something you bear together. But *won't*? Won't *try*? Will let you have one but will hold it against you for the rest of your life? It is not the same thing as *can't*.

I tell him that if you decide to do something for someone, you commit to that idea and you do it selflessly. You don't put your loving wife, who you claim to love in return, through all this. You don't hold her to ransom for it. You don't con her.

This ignites his nasty side again and he explodes ferociously. He goes through to the kitchen. I follow. He starts picking things up off the draining board, throwing the plastic utensils at the floor, bellowing. He gets closer and closer to my face, screaming and swearing, cornering me. I am desperately hoping that the neighbours will come round to see what's happening – perhaps someone else being alarmed by his behaviour will show him how extreme he's being? I'm surprised they haven't called the police. He won't stop yelling and the noise echoes through the house. The stepson is listening to music upstairs and I pray he cannot hear, that he doesn't come down and get hit by a flying utensil. I've already had a ladle-end in the face. The noise of his hatred booms in my head, and my heart is screeching for me to get out of the house. I beg him to stop but he won't. I'm shaking, I'm sweating and suddenly I am screaming too. My face is burning and red, just like the inside of my mind. I break free from my corner and bolt past him into the other room.

I don't know how it happens, it is not a moment I remember afterwards, but somehow I have a dining room chair in my hands. I lift it high into the air. It stays there for the briefest of moments, perfectly balanced as if suspended in time, before I bring it crashing down onto the floor. It breaks into a hundred pieces.

The screaming stops.

Silence.

For a moment I look at the piece I'm left brandishing and, for an even briefer moment, I'm quite cross that the chair didn't hold out better.

The carpenter stares blankly at me. I am glad that I haven't actually hit him. I wasn't wholly sure I didn't bring the chair down over his head. Realising what I have been pushed to, that I am standing here holding a stick of chair, and that I have actually broken our furniture, is a massive, life-changing moment for me. I almost smile, as the thought suddenly comes into my head that I must look like Valjean in *Les Miserables,* about to fend of Javert. But we are not fighting over the body of a dead Fantine. The body on the floor is our relationship.

I drop the baton and grab my car keys. I drive to my neighbour's house round the corner. She is not in. I drive to my best friend's house. She is not in either. I'm distressed, panicked. I need someone to help me, someone I can turn to. I am frightened and shocked and I need to talk it out. Or maybe be talked out of what I think I must do.

The carpenter doesn't call to see where I am. Nor does anybody else. He clearly hasn't realised that things are desperate, that we are in crisis. He doesn't know where I've gone. He isn't concerned and he doesn't try to find me.

I am sorry that I have broken the chair. I am ashamed that I have been pushed this far. I go back to the house after sitting in the parked car for ages. I go in and clean up the debris. I bring the spare chair down from the loft so the stepson will never know. The carpenter is drinking again, or maybe still... it's hard to say.

31st August

I cancel the IVF. I will not bring a child into the world with a father who refuses to be a parent. I will not have a child like this, with this person, on these terms.

14th September

There are days of nothingness. Of spare room sleeping, silent eating and letter-receiving numbness. I tell him that, unless something drastically changes, we have no future together, that I am done here. Venom hangs in the air. The stepson moves out.

Not long after the night of the dining room chair, the office call and say that they are scaling back. They're making me redundant. I think they've realised they can get by with unpaid interns doing my job, and with the economy the way it is I can't really blame them. This blow should be devastating, but after everything I've lost of late it barely registers, it's just another setback on a long list. I'll make a fresh start – I've done it before. They're giving me a glowing reference.

I get an interview straight away for a nice little job. I grab the chance with both hands. Another beginning. It is nothing fancy, nothing long-term, and the money is awful, but it is mine and I treasure it. I want to take it. I *need* to take it. The thought of not doing it makes me feel even more depressed than I already was. I need to get back on my own two feet. I need purpose, something to look forward to again. The job centre is pleased.

1st October

So here I am in east London, helping to renovate a pub

and turn it into a little theatre. How fitting. They liked me because I have all the skills. I'm a good PA and co-ordinator, I'm very organised, I know about building works *and* I'm interested in the arts. Plus I clean up at the end of the day.

It suits me. It's a funny little place, but it'll be nice once it's finished. There is so much to do. The place is being totally gutted, stripped right back and fitted out from the bare walls in. There are not that many of us on the project, so I'm really getting stuck in, and the physical doing of things is again being a bit of a lifesaver. It is going to be a slow project, but I like the lack of pressure and time constraints. Fortunately there are no floors that need sanding!

It is here that I meet him, the beautiful young man with a heart as big as a lion. He is a divine creature, with hair the colour of autumn wheat, which catches the sunlight as it pours through the many windows.

We talk a lot. He is charming and easy to get to know, with a generosity of spirit that I've rarely seen before. There is something so very beguiling about him. He is kind and has an intelligent turn of phrase that is both interesting and funny, bringing vibrancy to these draughty old rooms as he paints away, singing to himself. He makes everything feel otherworldly somehow, and his smile... his *smile*. It is when I'm with him that I soften, my past wisping away behind me. It is as if life is warm again and the air itself is filled with honey. You could almost get fat on it.

One day, we go for drinks after work and he walks me to the bus stop afterwards. Suddenly I can feel my heart racing through my coat, beating as if it will burst right through the lining. He hugs me goodbye and I blush, flustered. I daren't move. My head is on his chest by his heart, and it too is beating loudly, racing just like mine. And I know. In that moment I know. I've never felt anything like this before. We try to say goodbye but our silent mouths land side by side. We stay there for a moment, lost for words but, with no hope of walking away, he kisses me and the world falls away.

I go home. I pack a bag. I go downstairs.

There is another letter waiting for me. It is the carpenter who writes now. Great reams and reams of pleading, anger and confusion, and I daresay the next one will be full of regret.

For the last year, it's been me penning my thoughts, my heart marking the pages. Now it is him who writes: endless, awkward, unintelligible letters, words vomited onto the page that I can make little sense of. He seems desperate now and I am angry for that. Where was this fight before? Because now it is too late. Yesterday's letter was particularly upsetting. He asked: 'Why is it that no one ever loves me?' Is he kidding? I find it insulting. No one ever loved him? He must be blind.

I want to write my own letter in response, because I *did* love him. I loved him in spite of his faults and flaws, just like you're meant to. I looked past all the silly foolish things and I didn't judge, I saw the real person underneath, and I loved him. And yet he treated me like that. So it doesn't matter that I loved him. It doesn't matter. I want to ask my own question, except mine is rhetorical: 'Why is it that I loved someone so well and yet I was taken for granted and looked after as well as an old shoe? And why is it only when you come to bin those shoes that you realise how much you loved them, and you try desperately to resurrect them, but it's too late? They are battered, tired and worn and the holes in them are too big to mend.' That's what I want to ask. Why, how, when you love someone, do they treat you like that?

Maybe I am a fool to love and expect so little for myself in return. But then again, do I? I've left before haven't I?

The other husband treated me like an old shoe too. They both took out their own life frustrations on me, when I'd gladly given everything of myself to help them. I supported them and loved them through it all, and yet somehow I became the whipping post.

I know I can be tough and walk life on my own, but I want so much to be loved kindly and fully. And it hurts. The need for it physically hurts. The carpenter squandered my love and kicked it until it was flat and lifeless and gone.

The lady with the black cat had been right: 'Don't say yes to the first one.'

I tell him I'm leaving.

'Don't be daft,' he says, brushing me off as if I am an annoying fly. 'Where are you going to go? No one else will love you like I do.'

I want to tell him that, actually, I'm quite pleased about this. But I just stare at him.

'You never said you'd actually leave if I didn't treat you any better,' he says. He is drunk. He starts to panic. 'I'll change. I'll never drink again!' We both know that this is another lie. 'I'll put three back.' He means embryos. 'I'll read to our child, I'll be a good dad, I'll give you your dreams.'

At no point does he say he'll be a good husband.

I say nothing. I am done pleading. He should never have pushed me to this place. I'd never *pretend* to leave. It's a threat no one should ever have to make. And this isn't a threat. I am going.

I take a piece of paper and I write my last words to him. *How could I ever trust you?*

I leave. I do not know where I am going. But I know I cannot go through the rest of my life feeling the way I have done this last year. I cannot stay with someone who has done this to me.

I accept that it is over. Perhaps it should never have *been* in the first place, but for the first time in a long time I do not regret it, because it has brought me to here. A door has been opened and I want to walk through it, I *have* to walk through it. And on the other side? Hope. Time. My dreams. Myself. For, suddenly, I am *me* again. Not a number, not a hospital patient, not a housewife or a statistic. Me.

I must rewrite my life, starting now.

And I don't have to accept anyone else's version of what it should be... I am me.

Just me.

My name is Molly.

Acknowledgements

With thanks to Jason, Xanna and all at Big Finish.
Thanks also to my family, both close and extended;
Howard, Mum, Dad, Jenny, Jenna, Beth *et al* and my
wonderful family of friends, in particular Alistair, for
inspiration, problem solving and support always.

Also by the author

After the Break-Up: A Girl's Guide

What do you do when The One turns out not to be The One after all? When your dream home is snatched away from you, unfinished Schreiber kitchen units and all, and your dog is sent to live with your parents? When you suddenly have to find a flatmate, a way to pay the rent, a reason to keep going and maybe, ultimately... a new boyfriend?

Sharp, funny and hugely entertaining, Carrie Sutton charts her life in the year following the Big Break-Up. The bad dates... the good friends... the times when you think you can't go on... and the moment you realise you are finally OK on your own.

If you've experienced a Big Break-Up and need some cheering up, a bit of friendly advice and a few practical tips – then this is the book for you! Reading this book is like talking to your best friend over a large glass of wine. Uplifting, truthful and wise; as a feel-good remedy, it does everything except order you a cab home at the end of the evening!

'Carrie Sutton writes with style, wit and insight about a problem we've all had to face at some point in our lives. It's a must-read for those who've just come out of a relationship – a blueprint for survival for women and a lesson for men!' *Alistair McGowan*

Available now from bigfinish.com

After the
Break-Up:
A Girl's Guide

My year of

good friends,

bad dates

and new

underwear...

Carrie Sutton